Promise Me

Victoria Gemmell

Rusted Moon Press

First published in 2021 as Ebook and Print Edition
Text Copyright © Victoria Gemmell, 2021
https://victoriagemmell.com

Cover design © Rebecca Johnstone, 2021
https://daintydora.co.uk

Poetry Quotations - *The Raven* (1845) by Edgar Allan
Poe (Chapters 14, 15, 20, 21, 22)

ISBN: 978-1-7398110-0-6

Rusted Moon Press ☾

For readers everywhere- thank you

Promise Me

The Party: Scene One

It was Halloween and she was a ghost, dressed in a Victorian style nightdress, her bare feet peeking out from below the hem as she walked. Charcoal grey circled her eyes, her lips blood red.

Patrick whispered in her ear.

"You'd make a beautiful corpse."

Louise shuddered.

"Morbid. I'm a ghost; post corpse."

He poured more punch into her glass. "Would you come back to haunt me?"

"Maybe." Her lips formed a teasing smile.

Patrick wrapped an arm around her waist and nuzzled her neck.

His grip was strong, almost possessive.

A camera flashed in their faces and they blinked, caught off guard.

"Beautiful!" A magician shouted out, his rabbit waving beside him.

"Take one of us." The rabbit thrust the camera in their direction.

Patrick released Louise from his grip and reached for the camera. He tucked the Polaroid photo of them into his belt before turning to the magician.

Louise slipped away, side-stepping the hanging skeletons and watched as her classmates danced and laughed.

Her eyes were drawn to a boy standing alone in the corner of the room. A pirate; scarf tied around his head and beard drawn on, Captain Sparrow style. He looked uncomfortable, lost.

After a few minutes his gaze met hers, eyes a familiar blue.

Christian had come to her party?

She smirked, but didn't look away. His arms were folded and even beneath the wig and scarf she could tell he was frowning.

Always looking angry and disinterested; *what was his problem?*

He headed for the door. Louise moved forward, ignoring calls from a friend to come and dance.

Determination and curiosity sparked inside. From a young age, boys had always fawned around her; she never had to work hard. But with him…he always looked less than impressed. It bothered her.

Out in the hall she caught a glimpse of him at the top of the staircase. She followed silently, nightdress flowing out behind her, blonde curls tumbling down her back.

It was an image which haunted many, forming their last memory of her. A ghost climbing the stairs, walking to her death.

Chapter One

Mum crunched the gears all the way up the hill, the car almost rolling backwards on more than one occasion.

"Nearly there!" She shot me a manic grin and I turned my music up another notch.

As we stuttered past his old house, distinctive with its blue window frames, a familiar Nirvana riff filled my ears. Goosebumps darted up my arms. I'd read he was a fan of nineties grunge and he looked a bit like Kurt Cobain.

The numerous images from online forums were imprinted in my mind; messy dirty blonde hair and startling blue eyes. Thanks to Mum I was also a fan of nineties grunge. It made me feel an affinity with him when I had read about his trial.

"What're you staring at?" Mum pulled out one of my ear buds and I jumped, realising I had my nose pressed up against the glass.

"Christian Henderson's house."

It felt strange speaking his name, like I knew him.

Mum pursed her lips. "Yeah well, the family don't live there anymore."

I remembered reading he lived with his mum. People made a lot of the fact his father had left when Christian was young. Now I had something else in common with him.

I was conscious Mum kept shooting me sidelong glances.

"You remember what we talked about?" she said.

I sighed, wishing I hadn't pointed out his house or brought up his name. Mum hadn't reacted well when she'd stumbled across the clippings I'd collected about Christian's trial. She found them during our pre-move clear-out. She'd misinterpreted my interest in his case as an unhealthy obsession.

The day I took notice of Christian Henderson coincided with the week from hell. Before that, his name was background noise.

I barely registered the newspapers spread across the breakfast table at weekends, my head too full of my own carefree life to really notice or care about some boy from a well-to-do Scottish village accused of murdering a local girl at a party.

Then things started to fall apart at home. Mum and Dad sat me down, trying to explain what they didn't fully understand at the time; that their marriage was over. Dad moved out temporarily to give us all 'breathing space'. Ironically, it felt like I stopped breathing during that 'in-between time' of waiting for answers, waiting for Dad to come home. I was sleep-walking through classes in school, not talking to anyone, not eating.

Until one afternoon in Mr Bailey's English class, a photograph of Christian flashed up on the whiteboard, the headline, *Troubled teen, from a broken home, convicted of murder* jumping out at me.

Broken home.

I looked into Christian's eyes, detecting an echo of pain which resonated deep inside. It was what I feared most; having my sense of home ripped apart and having my security taken away.

Mr Bailey wanted us to study Christian's case, to look at the rhetoric surrounding the reports, and in particular the online coverage.

The online forums debating Christian's case were more personal than the newspapers, with anonymous postings from locals speculating about what had really happened. Mr Bailey wanted us to consider if it was possible these could have contributed to his guilt.

Would a judge really be able to determine if a jury had been completely immune to any coverage prior to the trial?

The deeper I had delved into Christian's troubled life, the more I forgot about my own. And the more I read about him, the stronger my belief had grown that something had gone wrong here; things didn't seem to add up and it bothered me. It made me wonder if he could be innocent.

"Darcy?"

Mum's voice brought me back to reality. I realised she was waiting for some reassurance.

"Don't worry. I remember my promise," I mumbled, clicking my music back on.

By the time Mum had made the connection that the murder had taken place in Rowantree, she had already fallen in love with our new flat. I managed to convince her she was over-reacting, with the promise that I would stop reading about Christian Henderson and forget about a horrible incident which happened long ago.

The car rolled to a stop.

"We're here." Mum turned to me, looking for approval.

I pulled out my ear buds and looked up at the flat complex. It was as swish as I remembered from the brief tour. Like something from Hollywood, minus the communal pool and sunshine.

My shoulder offered a half shrug.

"This is going to be a good thing, Darcy. A fresh start."

"Whatever." I sighed, leaning down to slip my

Converse back on.

"We're going to like it here. I'm sure of it." As I looked up I caught the plead in her eyes: *This is difficult enough for me, please don't make it any harder*. A pang of guilt numbed my resentment.

"It'll be great." I squeezed her hand quickly and opened the car door before she started to cry. Or worse, before I did. The air smelled different here, away from the pollution of inner-city Glasgow. This was what being rich must smell like.

Mum pulled out the kettle from the boot and a box of herbal tea. "Come to Mama!"

The big move had officially taken place last week. Dad insisted on flying up, taking time out from his new life in London to help. I chose to stay at gran's and go to my old school, to hand in overdue library books and say my goodbyes as everyone started their sixth year without me. Basking in the celebrity status that a last day incurred was much more attractive than making small talk with a man I no longer had any respect for.

"Race you!" Mum sped off up the path to our building, her auburn hair flowing out behind her.

"How old are you?" I shouted after her, running to catch up.

"Twenty-five," she yelled back.

"You wish!"

A girl opened the door to the building just as Mum reached the top step.

Mum nearly fell over, panting in her face. The girl recoiled, a look of disgust barely concealed.

Great. My face burned. *Fantastic first impression.*

The girl was beautiful in an intimidating way. Tall, curvaceous in the right places, masses of curly blonde hair. Every skinny red-haired girl's nightmare.

"Hi, I'm Lily and this is my daughter, Darcy." Mum slung an arm around my shoulders. "Your new neighbours."

A smirk played on the girl's lips.

"Welcome ...*Darcy*."

My cheeks burned as I mumbled a thanks.

"What's your name?" Mum prompted.

The girl looked taken aback by Mum's forwardness.

"Kara." She looked me up and down and I edged further up the stairs, uncomfortable with her scrutiny.

"Well, great to meet you, Kara. Have a lovely day."

Kara nodded in response and hurried down the stairs. As I watched her retreating mane of blonde curls, recognition dawned. *Kara Stephenson.*

"D'you know who that was?" I hissed as I followed Mum into the building. We started up the stone steps.

"A girl who got flippin' lucky when the puberty queen came to visit."

I smiled. "That was the dead girl's cousin."

Mum's shoulders visibly tensed and I braced myself, waiting for her to bring up my promise again.

"At least use her name, instead of referring to her as *the dead girl*."

Louise's name started to form on my lips just as Mum interrupted with, "Anyway, I thought she lived with Louise's family in the big house, does she not?"

I was surprised Mum knew that. She always shut down any conversation when I tried to read her bits about the trial from social media over breakfast.

"I think they all had to move out for a bit...due to forensic analysis. And press intrusion. Maybe Kara didn't want to move back in with them."

"Don't blame the poor girl." We reached the top floor and Mum lunged at our door. "Check it, check it." She framed our new name plaque with her hands.

"Lily and Darcy." I read the plaque with a frown. "Mum, you don't put our first names on it. The postie has to know our surname..."

My voice trailed off as I realised we no longer had the same surname – Mum was choosing to take back her maiden name, and I was staying a Thomas.

"But I'm sure they'll figure it out."

She was fumbling with the lock, thankfully not paying much attention.

The door creaked open, the smell of new carpets and IKEA furniture a depressing hello. I wandered into the living room and was relieved that it already started to look like home, with our favourite books lined up along wooden shelves and familiar paintings dotted around. Some new trinkets and throws on the sofas marked just enough change.

"So what d'you think, kid?" Mum hooked her arm around my waist, pulling me close.

I leaned my head against her shoulder.

"I think we're going to be a-okay.

Chapter Two

School was already a few weeks into the new term. Finlay Academy.

"Best reputation in the West of Scotland," Dad had said.

Such a great reputation that it had taken months of negotiation with the Council to let me in, particularly because my old High School was technically still within our catchment area.

Mum had been less than enthusiastic.

"She's moving into her last year – it's a stupid time to change school..."

"She's never had an easy time in that jungle of a school. There's nothing to challenge her there and she's always saying no one 'gets' her."

I stopped to listen out in the hall, surprised that Dad had actually picked up on my unhappiness at school.

"She's seventeen, Jim. No one is supposed *to get her."*

"Most of the young people from the village go to Finlay Academy. It'll be easier for her."

"It's the fact that most of the young people from the village go there that worries me. You know I found folders full of clippings about that boy, about the murder. She collected them for months. I'm worried if Darcy goes to his school, she'll get distracted again with it."

I held my breath, waiting for Dad's reaction. I knew how impressed he'd been when I showed him Finlay Academy's latest HMI inspection report online.

"The fact she got so involved in that English class debate about the case shows she needs stimulation," Dad said. "Isn't it a good thing she feels passionate about social justice?"

When Mum didn't react, Dad continued, "I just think going to the main catchment school will make it easier for her to settle in Rowantree."

"None of this is easy for either of us. Don't you think we've encountered enough change?" Mum's voice was getting shrill and I knew that signalled the start of a proper argument, or tears.

I pushed the door open. "I want to go. Please." They looked over at me in surprise.

Dad nodded. "I'll make it happen."

So, a few months of Dad's best persuasive talk and an offer to pay for a new computer lab and here I was.

A mix of anticipation and fear flashed up and down my legs as I climbed the stairs to reception. *This is an opportunity, Darcy, to impress. To live up to your name and be a freaking cool rocker with attitude.* I could leave the old boring Darcy behind at my other school and carve out a new life of excitement. The thought calmed my nerves.

"Watch it." A boy shoved past me through the doors, his bag clipping the side of my head.

I mumbled an apology, catching the door before it hit me in the face. A mass of purple blazers and noise sent the fear in my legs into overdrive.

No one glanced in my direction as I searched out the office, all too busy catching up on the weekend's gossip. Shiny haired girls laughed and huddled close. Not so much orange fake tan here; more of a subtle-tinted moisturiser. Good news for a freckled pale face.

The office staff shoved a timetable at me, a harassed-looking woman mumbling something about my pastoral care teacher dealing with some crisis so he'd meet with me another time. The bell rang and the noise levels peaked, a sea of bodies darting off in all directions.

I read my timetable.

"Where's the English department?"

"Turn left down the corridor. Advanced Higher class last on the right." The woman looked over my shoulder, turning her attention to the next person.

I stood to one side, waiting for the crowds to disperse then set off down the corridor. English was a good start to the day; better than Maths, for instance, which had the potential to induce panic and stupid answers. Words, and subjectivity, I could handle.

Through the open door I could see the class was mainly seated, the teacher handing out papers. She looked up at me and curious eyes followed her gaze.

"Yes?" She pushed her glasses up on top of her head.

"I'm Darcy. I'm new."

My voice sounded too loud in the silence.

"Why don't you give us a pirouette, *Darcy*."

I looked to the back of the class where Kara smirked, a couple of girls sniggering beside her.

"Zip it, Kara." The teacher motioned to a desk at the front of the class. "Take a seat, Darcy."

I sank into the chair, avoiding eye contact with the boy beside me. As I laid my notebook on the desk a name carved in the wood caught my eye. I traced a finger over the letters; *Christian*. He'd sat in this seat, or at least at this desk.

"Are you named after the ballet dancer?" the boy beside me asked, without looking up. He'd written his name at the top of his paper: *Daniel.*

"No. The bass player from the Smashing Pumpkins."

"Cool." He nodded and I waited for him to say something else. He didn't.

A copy of *To Kill A Mockingbird* was placed on my desk and I started to relax into the lesson, though couldn't shake the sensation that Kara was watching me from behind, analysing my every move.

The door swung open and heads darted up.

"Morning." A tall, arrogant-looking boy sauntered in, giving the teacher a wave. *Patrick Barrington.*

"Twenty minutes late, Patrick. I'm not impressed."

"Sorry, Mrs C. I'll try harder tomorrow."

He flashed her a grin. A few of the girls giggled.

"Asshole," Daniel muttered under his breath.

Patrick stopped at my desk and at first, I thought he'd heard Daniel. But his attention was on me, a teasing smile playing on his lips.

"Well, hello, new girl."

Disarming, more than capable of deception. It was the picture I had built of him when I'd read some stories about him during the trial. Looking into his eyes sent a shiver down my spine.

And then I heard a little voice whisper somewhere deep inside: *This boy should not be trusted.*

*

Lunchtime arrived; a welcome but at the same time dreaded part of the day. Where to sit? Where to go? A glance through the open door of the canteen revealed mayhem; long queues, screeching laughter, reserved seats at overflowing tables. Kara and Patrick and a petite brunette headed the queue, so I kept walking. My timetable was weirdly in sync with Kara's, apart from Psychology, and she hadn't made much attempt so far to make me feel welcome. The other girls seemed to be following suit by barely acknowledging my existence. So much for making a great first impression.

Sunshine streamed in the windows, persuading me to venture outside. A large oak tree was firm in my memory from my walk through the gates that morning; a perfect resting spot to sit and eat my packed lunch, listen to some tunes, catch up on some reading. *Geek,* an inner voice shouted. "Shut up," I mumbled.

"What?"

I blinked in surprise and looked up to see Daniel pushing the main doors open in front of me.

"Nothing." I grabbed onto the straps of my backpack, embarrassed.

"Where you off to?" he asked, holding the door for me.

I shrugged. "Just outside."

He looked at me curiously, like he was trying to decide if I was a bit soft in the head.

"How about you?" I asked.

He tucked a strand of black hair behind his ear and I caught a flash of a star tattoo on the inside of his wrist, partly obscured by the cuff he wore. "Going to sit on the grass. You can join me if you want."

"Okay. Thanks."

We walked side by side in silence along the gravel path, down to the grassy verge beyond the car park. A few boys were kicking a ball about and girls were lying on the grass, making the most of a fluke late summer.

"Hey, Daniel."

We both turned at the voice, my eyes registering the spark of flirtation in the smile belonging to the girl with black and blue hair. Her tie hung loose like she was making a point that she refused to be restricted, her skirt skimming the top of her bare thighs, violet eyes lined with dark kohl which gave her pretty pixie features a hard edge. She cocked her head in my direction, her nose stud winking in the sunlight.

"Who are you?" Her forwardness made me self-conscious and I felt my cheeks scorch as I introduced myself, telling her it was my first day and that I had just moved to Rowantree, wishing my mouth would stop moving and let me play it cool.

The girl raised an eyebrow. "Poor you. It's probably the most boring place on earth." I wondered if she meant Finlay Academy, or the village, or both.

I waited for her to return the introduction, but then her phone beeped and she laughed at whatever message filled her screen and she walked off without saying goodbye.

"Who was that?" I asked, simultaneously enchanted and affronted by her rudeness.

"That's Roo. She's Zoe's little sister. Zoe's in our year; she was sitting with Kara in English."

I nodded, names already listed in my head, matching to new faces.

Little sister. I looked over my shoulder, watching Roo's retreating back, taking in her confident stride. She was small and skinny, sure, but her aura suggested Senior. "What year is she in?"

"Fourth." Daniel shot me a wry smile. "She's trouble."

Daniel led me past the crowds and set his bag down at a quiet spot. He threw himself onto the ground and stretched out.

"I hate this place so much."

I sat crossed legged beside him. "It seems okay. Better than my old school anyway."

"Where did you go?"

"Linton High. Not far from here."

He sat up, letting out a low whistle. "You must be well hard."

I smiled wryly. "Yeah, as you can see, I'm all muscle."

He laughed. "How come you started here?"

"Thought it would be good to make a complete fresh start." I pulled at the grass, noticing that Daniel wore tight black jeans in favour of the cotton trousers all the other boys seemed to be wearing. "D'you live in the village?"

"Yeah, our own little celebrity jungle," he scoffed, and I knew he was referring to the way in which the press had invaded the village for the past couple of years.

"It's weird because I feel like I sort of know Kara and Patrick," I said slowly, unsure about how much anyone would want to talk about things.

"You don't," he said sharply, his expression darkening. "You can never trust what you read on the internet. I bet you think you know Christian too." His green eyes were challenging, defensive.

"Were you friends with him?"

As I asked the question, I realised that Daniel was the 'best friend' who had tried to defend him on numerous occasions in forums.

Daniel nodded, throwing a stone at a tree up ahead. "And it still makes me so mad, the way everyone totally sold out on him. He never stood a chance."

"So, you think he's innocent?" I asked, pulling my lunch out from my bag, watching Daniel's face closely.

"No question. There is no way Christian is a murderer. He's not a violent person. He couldn't do something like that; slapping Louise across the face, then stabbing her."

The image made me shudder.

"For what it's worth I couldn't believe it when he was found guilty. It seemed wrong," I said quietly, biting into my sandwich.

Daniel frowned. "Which part of the social media hounding gave you that impression?"

"Some of the stories, the way they wrote about him – like just because he was quiet and a bit aloof, they made out like he was a weirdo. I mean, obviously I don't know him."

A piece of chicken sandwich stuck in my throat as I met Daniel's scrutinising gaze.

Daniel folded his arms. "Did you follow the whole trial?"

I hesitated, thinking back to the days following that introduction to Christian's case in Mr Bailey's English class. I hadn't been aware of the trial when it played out in real-time; we were looking back on everything, just after Christian's conviction. Then I had spent hours trying to piece together the story, wondering what had really happened the night of the party. The online debaters attempted to build a profile of who Christian really was, speculating about his motivations, bringing his Mum into the conversation; the outspoken hippie outcast with wild eyes and wild hair adding fire to suspicions that 'something wasn't quite right' about the family, just because they didn't fit the standard affluent middle-class profile of most of the villagers.

It was the motivation part I was most fascinated

by. And all of the unanswered questions about the young people who might have played a part that night. I looked at Daniel, wondering what he really knew. What part might he have played? "Not in any major depth. Some stories stick in my head more than others. And some people."

Daniel's expression softened, a desperation flickering beneath the defensiveness, like he needed someone else to believe in his friend.

I thought back to the forums I'd read, the 'case analysis' podcasts that supposedly-intelligent local adults and students had set up, the anger I'd felt at some of the sensationalised coverage of someone so young. Mr Bailey was an ex-journalist and he explained to us that the press had also exploded with pictures two months after his arrest, in March 2015 when Christian had turned sixteen.

Mr Bailey seemed angry, like me, about the way the papers had vilified Christian, fuelled by witch-hunt-style commentators on social media. Our class debate got cut short when the head of the English department suggested we focus on less sensitive discussions in class, and I never did find out if Mr Bailey thought Christian was innocent. I knew Mr Bailey would be pleased the law in Scotland had changed just a few months after Christian's conviction, meaning no one under the age of eighteen could be named in the press for a crime, but I wondered how much control anyone could ever have over the social media forums, or the local gossip in the village shop and pub which blackened names and cemented reputations.

I considered telling Daniel about our discussion, but decided it might just get him worked up. Instead I shared one of my thoughts I'd voiced during the class.

"The impression I got of Christian, was that he was misunderstood. He came across as perceptive and quite literal, which probably did him no favours."

"What do you mean?" Daniel sat up.

I hesitated, wondering if I should try to cut the conversation short. It was obvious Daniel's feelings were still a bit raw about the whole thing. "Well... if you're good at seeing someone for who they really are but no one else can, then it makes you appear like a judgemental ass, right?"

Daniel nodded. He let out a long sigh. "You're right about him being misunderstood. He wasn't great at socialising – he was an outcast here but not in a shunted kind of way. Most of the time it was him choosing to evade others, not them rejecting him. That literal way he had of communicating that you picked up on...it made him come across as a bit insensitive but really I think he's the complete opposite." Daniel flushed. He made a face and tensed his arms into a muscle man stance. "Not like me, Mr Macho man."

I laughed to help defuse his embarrassment, desperate to leave with at least one friend today. I didn't want Daniel clamming up on me now.

"And he was very talented of course. At art," I added. Sketches of Louise's face flashed through my mind. Someone at the party had found sketches of Louise in the bag Christian had left behind and had handed them into the police, allowing people to build a picture of obsession. I asked Daniel what he made of that.

"He acknowledged that she was aesthetically pleasing but he didn't like her. He thought she was stuck up," Daniel said grimly.

She was pretty when she didn't talk. A quote

which was distorted and turned against him when he expressed an honest opinion of a pretty girl he had no time for.

Daniel held out his hand to me. I hesitated and he smiled. His handshake was firm.

"So, I think we can be friends now."

I returned the smile, relieved I'd made at least one good impression today.

Daniel lay back down on the grass. "Man, I miss him."

"D'you ever visit him?"

"At the start I did. But now he keeps telling me not to."

"Why?" I tried to imagine what it would feel like to be locked away, cut off from everyone I loved. I would cling on to any contact I could.

"Because the offenders' unit sucks big time. He tells me to pretend that he's on tour with Aerosmith."

I laughed and Daniel smiled.

"I email him."

"He gets access to email?" I realised I knew nothing about prison or a young offenders' unit. Only images from films and TV programmes of traditional prisons, which probably wouldn't reflect the unit Christian was in. But I bet he didn't have a window. Not being able to look out and see the sky, see the world – that would drive me insane.

"Sort of. I can email him through a prison email system, but he can't email back so he writes me letters. Sometimes." Daniel made a face. "He doesn't write much but I feel like I have to keep him connected to reality, you know? I worry he's going to lose it in there. I would totally lose it. We talk on the phone sometimes too, but he's always hated talking on the phone so prefers to write."

I stopped myself from asking more, not wanting to push things with Daniel.

"He gets a lot of mail from girls who think he's innocent."

"Oh yeah?" I asked, surprised.

Daniel grinned. "I don't think it's based on the fact they've done any investigative analysis. More about aesthetic analysis and no doubt wanting to rescue 'the bad boy'."

My face flushed, hoping my defending of his character hadn't come across like that.

"Where you staying in the village?" Daniel asked, changing the subject.

"In the flat complex on Kyle Road."

"They're quite posh. Kara must be your neighbour then?"

"Yeah. She's in my building. Didn't she used to live with...the Marshalls?" I didn't feel comfortable saying Louise's name in front of him; it sounded over familiar and Daniel was already touchy about me acting like I knew them all.

"Kara never went back to that house after the murder. She lives with her gran now."

"What about her parents? Where are they?"

"In France. Story goes she'll move out to be with them once she's finished school. She spent the summer out there. I was surprised she came back for a sixth year. But I've heard rumours that her parents aren't the best, which is why she was living with the Marshalls. Think her Mum has some problems with alcohol, and her Dad didn't seem to be around much."

"Oh."

I started to see Kara in a new light. No wonder she came across as a bit abrasive.

The bell rang and Daniel grabbed his bag,

jumping to his feet. "What you in next?"

"Art, I think."

"Cool. Me too."

We walked through the crowds, returning inside to the madness.

"You'll like Mr Harris. He's about the only decent teacher in this dump," Daniel said as we climbed the stairs to the art department. "He also really stuck up for Christian."

"Only because he was sleeping with his mum."

I jumped at the voice behind us. I turned in time to see Kara's frown before she disappeared around the corner to the Science department. I was relieved that she wasn't joining us in Art.

"Is that true?" I asked Daniel.

"They became close during the investigation. Christian's mum wasn't exactly supported locally, whereas Mr Harris was completely on their side. Kara's just bitter about it because she felt like it was a betrayal to Louise."

Daniel shoved open the Art room door and the smell of turpentine and paint was comfortingly familiar. The desks were set out in a circle, with tables in the centre littered with weird and wonderful objects. A tall man with spiky greying hair and a bright red shirt stood at the back of the room, rinsing paint brushes. He was humming along to the tune blasting from the stereo. It was one Mum loved…and one I secretly liked too, even although I complained it was so depressing any time she played it in the car. The teacher turned to smile at me just as the singer's name popped into my head; *Morrissey*.

I sat down next to Daniel and glanced round the class, noting some new faces. Kara's brunette friend sat across the room. *Zoe*. She was quieter than the others. And much less 'in your face' than her sister, Roo.

"Hey, new girl."

A cloud of aftershave invaded my nostrils as Patrick slid onto the stool at my other side.

"It's your lucky day," he grinned. "Thought we should get to know one another better."

"Yeah, lucky me," I said, my heart sinking. I caught Zoe watching us.

She quickly looked away when our eyes met. The seat beside her was vacant and I wondered if Patrick usually sat there.

I jumped as Daniel's stool scraped back.

"Where're you going?" I hissed.

"I'm not sitting anywhere near him," Daniel said, gathering up his things. I watched in disbelief as he wandered across to the other end of the room, sliding onto the stool beside Zoe. My face burned.

Patrick let out a low whistle. "Rude, eh?"

I didn't answer.

"Don't let him give you the wrong impression. I'm a nice guy, really. You'll see that when you get to know me." He flashed me a dazzling smile; the kind that could convince girls of anything if they were gullible enough.

But when his smile faded there was darkness in his eyes, hinting that something deeper was hidden beneath the charm. That was the Patrick I was curious about, even if every fibre of my body warned me to stay away.

Chapter Three

"Mr Barrington, I hope you plan to do some work today and not harass this young lady." Mr Harris walked past us, shooting me a small smile. He dropped a piece of paper in front of Patrick. "C minus for your homework sketch."

I observed his drawing; a stick man with a distorted rectangular face, smoking a cigar.

"It's abstract art, Mr Harris. You were just saying last week how underrated it is."

"Nice to know that you listen to some of what I say."

"About fifty per cent," Patrick shot back and some of the class sniggered. He slid his drawing in front of me, lowering his voice. "What do you think, Darcy?"

I tensed, uncomfortably aware of how close his hand was, our fingers nearly touching. "I think he could do with a good feed."

Patrick's blue eyes sparked. "Maybe I should draw him a woman so she can cook him dinner."

I shot him a withering smile.

"So, when did you move to Rowantree?" He moved his hand away and I relaxed a bit.

"Just a few days ago," I said.

"You're in my girlfriend's building, right?"

I blinked in surprise. "Kara?"

"Yeah, Kara. The one and only."

I wondered when they'd started going out and what Louise's parents would think of their niece dating their late daughter's boyfriend. A boyfriend who the police had spent time questioning for her murder.

Mr Harris circled the room, talking about light and shadow, laying out chalks and charcoal. He stopped at my desk. "Take your time settling into things, Darcy. Did you study National Art?"

I nodded. His eyes shone with an inquisitive youthfulness, like life hadn't worn him out yet.

"So why did you move here?" Patrick continued when Mr Harris moved on.

I hesitated. "My parents are getting divorced."

"Bummer. I sometimes wish my parents would get divorced."

"Why?"

He shrugged. "The arguments."

I wanted to tell him that at least the arguments would prepare him, that maybe when one of his parents did walk out it wouldn't feel like he'd suddenly woken up in someone else's life.

Patrick steered the conversation onto other topics, grilling me about my personal life, particularly boyfriends. I chose to answer evasively, refusing to admit to this ego maniac that I was yet to have a proper boyfriend.

I tried to catch Daniel's attention. He was intently sketching and Zoe caught me looking. She shot me a small smile. I smiled back, surprised. Maybe not all of the girls thought I was a loser.

The period passed quickly. I jumped up as soon as the bell rang, hurrying over to Daniel before he reached the door.

"Thanks for ditching me and leaving me with Mr Perfect Hair." I growled.

"Sorry. I just can't stand being near him. Not after everything."

He didn't need to explain what he meant by 'everything'. Christian's account of the murder at the party placed Patrick at the scene after he'd left, something which Patrick flatly denied. It didn't take a genius to figure out who Daniel believed was the true guilty one.

"Darcy?"

I turned at Mr Harris's call.

Daniel touched my shoulder. "You got Maths next?"

I nodded, making a face. "Just National."

"I'm in Advanced Higher. I'll save you a seat on the bus after."

"Alright, catch you then." I waved.

I walked towards Mr Harris, my eyes drawn to the tattoo curling out from beneath his short-sleeved shirt. It seemed wrong seeing a teacher with a tattoo; it humanised him too much. I imagined teacher training would stipulate no visible tattoos. Maybe it did and he liked to break the rules.

"Take a seat, Darcy." He gestured to the stool beside him and I perched uncertainly. No other teachers had given me a welcome talk, which I hoped this was and not some analysis of my pathetic first attempt drawing with chalk and charcoal.

"Mr Barrington appears to have taken a shine to you."

My face flushed. "I think he just likes to show off – and I'm the new girl so maybe I'll hold his attention for another couple of days at least."

Mr Harris raised an eyebrow. "Or maybe just for today if you're lucky."

I grinned.

"On a more serious note though, just in case his attention becomes more...prolonged, you just let me know if it makes you uncomfortable."

I nodded, not knowing how else to respond. The

warning did nothing to ease my instincts that all was not sweetness and light with Patrick.

"Daniel is a good kid. You should stick with him." He stood up, indicating he was bringing our conversation to a close. "I don't know how much you know about what went on around here, but Daniel has really struggled the past while. It would be good for him to have someone to confide in. He's angry with a lot of people."

"His anger must be nothing compared to Christian's."

The words were out before I censored them. *Too personal, Darcy. You don't know these people.*

A flicker of surprise crossed Mr Harris's face. "So, Daniel has spoken to you about him? He's managed to get you on side pretty quickly."

"I was already on his side before I got here," I said.

"I see." Mr Harris stroked his chin, looking at me in wonder. "You'd better get to your next class, Darcy."

I picked up my bag, sensing his curious gaze following me to the door.

*

The house was too quiet when I arrived home. I turned up the stereo and collapsed onto the sofa, my head spinning with new names, faces, subjects. Part of me wanted to run back to my old life, but that wasn't an option. My old school and house were still there but Dad wasn't. It could never be the same.

My phone beeped and Dad's name flashed up.

Hi honey, hope your first day was okay. Call me later if you want. I'll be home by seven. Love Dad.

I threw my phone down to the end of the sofa. It was like he had a sixth sense or something. Every time I felt a surge of anger for him he made contact, like he was trying to deflect it. *It's not working, Dad.*

The kitchen was a better distraction. Four-thirty. Mum would be home in an hour, so I could start to make dinner. I opened the fridge.

A pint of milk, cheese, yoghurts, big bar of dairy milk, a couple of cans of Diet Coke and two carrots. The cupboards didn't fare any better; a box of Weetabix and Frosties, three tins of soup, half a loaf of bread, plain pasta, rice and some soy sauce. Mum had insisted on going shopping alone yesterday to give me time to unpack and settle in. Big mistake.

If Dad had done the shopping the fridge would be full of delicious food and he'd have promised to make me his infamous lasagne after my first day of school. The thought of never seeing Dad standing cooking in the family kitchen again sent a wave of grief and nausea shooting through me.

I blinked back tears, slamming the cupboard doors shut. I scrolled down my phone, wanting to call someone but not knowing who. Fee? She hadn't been responding to many of my messages and it would just make me miserable, hearing her talk about new things I was no longer part of. We'd already started to grow apart, and I knew my chat about Christian's case had started to bore her. She couldn't understand my fascination with it, or why I listened to True Crime podcasts. The desire to piece together puzzles was addictive.

I'd read articles where 'experts' tried to unpick why females in particular were drawn to True Crime stories, with a common depressing theory it helped us 'prepare' and understand the clues to look for, in case we found ourselves in dangerous situations. That chain of thought wasn't a conscious driving factor for me. I just liked the idea of uncovering things others had missed, which in a lot of ways made me sound like a narcissistic weirdo.

I walked down the hall to my room, stopping to move a box out the way. I hesitated, remembering I had hidden the folders about Christian's trial in one of them. I started to dig through the contents, finally finding a large folder in the last box. As I pulled it out, the ringed spine popped open, sending print-outs from Christian's 'trial' flying across the carpet. I bent to gather up the cuttings, my eyes drawn to the sensational headings from forums: *Dejected loner main suspect. Troubled teen had sinister obsession with pretty girl. Beautiful girl slain by demon outcast.* It was stories we'd looked at as part of the English class debate.

The haunted face of Christian Henderson stared back at me, his eyes and mouth unsmiling in later photographs, snapped by people who hounded his moves. His mum appeared in many of the pictures, attempting to shield her son, angry face like a protective lioness.

She had channelled some of that anger into conversations with local news stations, claiming a tight circle of the social elite within the village were targeting her son because he didn't fit into their 'prissy stuck-up world'. There was backlash from the Marshalls, who revealed unflattering accounts of Mrs Henderson appearing drunk at their doorstep, begging them to help her son, to support his innocence and help her find the 'real killer'.

I ran my finger over the words, *Dejected loner.* Since Dad left I'd felt a sense of being disconnected, not just from Fee, but other friends. I had become a bit of a loner too, tuning out of their care-free chatter, feeling there were more important things to worry about. I looked back at the photograph of Christian. "I bet you'd understand how I feel," I whispered.

I jumped, a banging catching my attention. There was a gap between songs on the stereo and I realised it was someone knocking on the door. I quickly shoved the files back into the folder, placing it back inside the box.

"Coming!"

I ran back into the living room, grabbing the remote to mute the music.

I opened the door, taken aback to find Kara holding what looked like a casserole in her hands, her face unsmiling.

"Hi," I said, eyeing the dish. Had she really brought me a welcome dinner?

"My gran thought I should bring you a 'welcome to the village' type present. She watches too many suburban American soaps on TV."

My lips twitched, wanting to smile, but a part of me didn't want to make it easy for the ice queen.

Kara glanced over my shoulder, eyes scanning the living room, her expression a mixture of curiosity and judgement.

"That was really nice of her, thanks." I took the dish and there was an awkward silence as we stood looking at one another.

"Zoe told me you were sitting next to Patrick in Art."

Oh, great. "*He* sat next to me, yeah." I hoped she'd heard where I put the emphasis, though I wasn't sure that would really help matters.

She looked me up and down. "Yeah, well. Don't

get too cosy."

I laughed. "You have nothing to worry about, trust me."

"I know that." Her scathing look filled in the unspoken words: *like he would fancy you.*

"Well, say thanks to your gran for the dinner, Kara."

She stepped back, smiling sweetly. "See you tomorrow, Darcy."

"Can't wait," I mumbled, kicking the door shut. I tilted the lid of the pot, giving it a cautious sniff.

My tummy rumbled at the delicious aroma of beef casserole. A part of me was tempted to eat it all now and leave Mum with Frosties for dinner.

I un-muted the stereo and carried the stew through to the kitchen, singing along to the music, trying to shake off the feeling of dread at Kara's warning about Patrick. She seemed less than impressed with me already, without this added into the mix. I started on washing up the breakfast dishes to calm my nerves. Mum was anxious I made new friends, so at least I hit it off with Daniel. He was easy to be around.

Mum burst through the front door, joining in the singing at the top of her voice. She hurried through to the kitchen, grabbing me by the waist, spinning me round. I tried to resist but she held on tight, singing in my face, making me laugh.

"Stop, please," I gasped, trying to catch my breath.

She stepped back, turning her attention to the casserole. "My, my. What is this?"

"That new school taught me to cook in one day. Can you believe it?"

Mum arched an eyebrow, surveying me for a moment. "No," she eventually said, laughing.

"Maybe not so unlikely if you'd actually bought some proper food to cook with, Mother dear," I said, wondering if the dig would register. "Kara's gran cooked it for us."

"Who?" She pulled a fork out from one of the drawers and started to attack the meat. I slapped her hand.

"Hey, no stealing bits." I stretched up to get plates. "That girl we saw the other day – you know, the one with the killer curves. *Her* gran. I wouldn't be surprised if she put some poison in it, mind you."

"Who, the gran?" Mum frowned.

"Noooo, Kara. Let's just say I don't think she likes me much."

Mum hugged me from behind. "Aw, how could anyone not love my little Darcy?"

I smiled, shaking my head. "How was your day at the library?"

"Alright. The girls told me to leave early as they knew it was your first day. It's a bit rubbish having a longer drive. Not sure if little Wanda will survive the winter months."

"I'm sure Dad will gladly buy you a new car. Help ease his guilt a little bit more." The bitterness seeped into my voice, flowing through me, leaving a bad taste in my mouth.

"Darcy."

The smile disappeared from Mum's face. "I don't want you feeling like this. Your dad isn't the enemy."

"How can you say that?" I folded my arms, trying to contain the anger I could feel simmering.

"I've told you before." She pinched my cheek. "Relationships are complicated. It's not all black and white."

The black was clear for me to see.

Dad was now living with his twenty-seven-year-old Personal Assistant in London, leaving me and Mum behind, with Mum desperate for me not to hate him. It made me hurt for her even more.

"So, what's the goss from school then?" she asked, filling up the kettle, the subject of Dad closed for now.

"Same old people in different disguises," I said. "Uch, not really. Most of the people seem alright. I met a cool boy..."

"Oooh, a boooy," Mum cooed, poking me in the side.

I rolled my eyes. "Not like that."

Not long after my fifteenth birthday Mum sat me down one day to announce that she had looked up an A-Z list of sexualities and was a bit perplexed to find at least twenty-nine but was open to conversations about any path I felt I wanted to take.

I told her I was pretty sure I was on the straight path, but would let her know if there were any deviations. Since then, she often enquired about any potential first boyfriends. Two years later I wondered if she was disappointed for me that there was still no sign of one.

"But is he good looking?"

Daniel's face flashed through my mind; chiselled jaw, prominent cheek bones. "Yes, actually. And he's a friend of Christian Henderson."

Mum's shoulders visibly tensed. She turned to look at me. "Well, I'm not sure I'm happy with you hanging around with him then, Darcy."

"Are you serious?"

She turned back to pouring our tea. "The girls in the library were talking about Christian Henderson today, because they know we've moved here. The way that poor girl was murdered, stabbed at a party. I mean, he must be one messed up kid to do that – only fifteen at the time. It sends chills down my spine."

"But you know I think Christian's innocent, Mum. After talking to Daniel today, I think so even more. And my art teacher thinks he's innocent too..."

"Darcy." Mum's tone was wary.

"Do you know how wrong the so-called 'justice' system can get things? How many innocent people in America get put on death row?"

I thought back to the documentaries I had watched about the West Memphis Three boys, my anger sparking.

"This isn't America, Darcy," Mum snapped. "You know nothing about Christian Henderson. And it's best to leave it that way."

"It just bothers me that someone so young could be wrongly convicted."

We stood looking at each other, the frown lines on Mum's forehead deepening.

I knew she would be worrying I was going to isolate myself again, like I had when Dad was in the process of moving out permanently, choosing to watch endless crime focused documentaries, getting lost in other peoples' stories.

I had attempted to get Fee to come with me to a Howard League Scotland lecture on promoting Civil Rights, but she'd looked at me like I'd grown two heads, so I'd gone alone. I'd felt a bit out of place, and lots of the discussion didn't really make sense to me, but it spurred me on, seeing so many people focused on the importance of justice. A lot of older adults shot me curious glances, clearly pleased and pleasantly surprised someone my age had bothered to come along.

Mum's expression softened, and she moved towards me, cupping my cheek. "I do admire your passion, Darcy. I really do. But this is not your case to fight. I want you to enjoy yourself here, make some new friends, have some fun."

"Daniel is a new friend," I mumbled.

Mum relented, "Well, just be careful around him, promise?"

I shrugged half-heartedly, not promising anything.

The Party: Scene Two

Louise found Christian in her parents' room, out on the balcony smoking a cigarette. He looked content, standing gazing up at the sky. As she watched him take a drag, she realised how attractive he was.

"You're not allowed in this room." Her voice came out whinier than intended.

Christian turned around slowly, strands of his pirate wig blowing in the wind. "I'm not in the room. I'm outside."

Always a smart-ass comment for everything.

"But you walked through it to get here." The cold air sent a shiver through her body as she stepped out to join him. "Can I get one?" She nodded towards his cigarette.

He reached into his pirate waistcoat pocket and threw the pack to her without looking.

She had to lunge forward to catch it.

"You got a light?"

This time he met her eyes briefly, then passed over an expensive-looking gold lighter.

"Thanks." She turned it over in her hand. His initials were engraved on the back: *CH*. "Was this a present?"

"Not exactly." He threw his cigarette to the ground and stubbed it out with the heel of his boot.

She took a slow drag on hers, watching him, waiting to see if he'd expand on his answer. Most boys she spoke to never shut up, always tripping over their words, throwing in self-indulgent stories to impress.

Patrick was always boasting about something.

This was new - having to work to dig out information, keep the conversation flowing.

The moon shone brightly, almost full. He seemed more interested in the sky than her. What was wrong with him?

"I'm surprised you came tonight," she said, positioning herself so that he had a good view of her dress. Surely, he couldn't be immune to her curves. Most of the boys downstairs hadn't been able to take their eyes off her all night.

"Me too. This is the last place I want to be."

Her cheeks burned at his bluntness. "Why did you come then?" She thought back to when she'd seen him in the park earlier that day, tempted to mention what she'd seen.

He shrugged. "Daniel persuaded me. He has a thing for Halloween; loves dressing up and all that."

"Well, you've made an alright effort yourself, Mr Jack Sparrow."

"I'm not trying to be Johnny Depp," he said, frowning. "I'm just a pirate."

He was clearly not susceptible to flirtation; she should just walk away now, stop wasting her time with this weirdo. But there was something annoyingly alluring about him. Those eyes, so intense - like there was something going on in there that might be worth sticking around to hear.

He stepped away from the balcony rail and turned towards the open doors.

"Your parents have a turntable."

Following his gaze, she noticed an old-fashioned player in the corner of the room, a stack of LPs in the open cabinet below.

"My dad likes to restore old players and jazz them up." She threw her cigarette to the ground and wandered inside, laying his lighter on the cabinet as she flicked through the LPs. "What kind of music d'you like?"

"What have they got?" He crouched down beside her and started to search from the opposite side.

"There's a lot of weird hippie music here and Seventies punk. My dad likes that kind of music."

She watched him curiously. His dad, as far as she knew, was no longer around. They must still be in touch though, for him to know what he listened to.

Something in his face softened as he searched through the music, like he was zoning out to a happy place.

"ABBA - let's put this on," he smiled, holding up the record.

"ABBA? Are you serious?" She couldn't tell if he was pulling her leg.

"Don't you like them?" He laid the record down onto the player, carefully positioning the needle onto the vinyl so that it crackled into life.

"I do, I just didn't think you would. I thought you'd be into cooler stuff."

"I like all sorts. The old stuff is good." He jumped back to sit on the bed and swung his legs in time with *Dancing Queen*.

She couldn't help but smile at the strangeness of the scene. A grunge pirate boy sitting on her parents' bed listening to a camp ABBA song.

She started to move to the music, singing along, getting louder the more she danced. His lips twitched with a half-smile.

"You don't smile much," she called above the music.

"Neither do you," he shot back.

This made her stop for a moment, trying to think

about how she acted around school. "I don't?"

"Not really," he said. "You always look kind of superior, like you're above smiling or something. Or maybe you're not that happy."

"Same back at you, Mr-I'm-Too-Good-To-Talk-To-Any-Of-You." She made a face at him as she spun round the other way. His words, saying she might not be happy, bothered her. Lately it felt like she was always trying too hard, like she was craving attention from the wrong people. Like Patrick. She blinked away tears.

"I think you should dance with me, Christian Henderson." She walked towards him, hands on hips.

"No way." He held up his hands in protest. "I don't dance."

"Come on." She grabbed his hand, pulling hard. "Just one dance."

"No." He shook his head, resisting her grip.

She dropped his hand and pouted. "Please," she cooed, fluttering her eyelashes. "Pretty please."

He rolled his eyes and jumped up. "Alright, if it'll stop you whining."

She clapped her hands in delight. "But let's put this song back to the beginning. It's the best one to dance to."

"Alright." He adjusted the needle and the song started over. She shot him a reassuring grin and he swung his arms, shuffling his feet.

"Loosen up a bit." She tapped his arms and wiggled her hips in demonstration.

"Why did I come here?" he groaned to the ceiling, moving his arms some more.

She could see a half smile playing on his lips and it made her happy that he seemed to be warming to her. "Spin me round."

She grabbed his hand and twirled beneath his arm. "See, you *can* dance." A surge of affection washed through her as she remembered back to when they were younger, when they were all friends and she didn't care so much about what anyone thought.

Christian tightened his grip on her hand and twirled her faster, round and round. As the room spun into a kaleidoscope of colours she laughed, unable to remember the last time she'd felt so free.

Chapter Four

"Gawd, Darcy. This place still looks like a bring-and-buy sale. And I stubbed my toe on those boxes *again*," Mum shouted on her way past my open door, munching angrily on toast and jam.

"Sorry, I meant to put them away last night." It was too early in the morning to endure Mum's nags, so I dragged the last box of belongings from the hall into my bedroom with a loud sigh, ignoring her protests that she didn't expect me to tidy *right now*.

As I dragged the box across my room the lid fell off and the folder caught my attention again. I slid down onto the floor, reading through more extracts and transcripts from podcasts. The stories seemed even more intriguing and awful now that I had spoken to one of Christian's close friends. As I read through them in more detail I realised there were so many questions that hadn't been properly answered. I thought back to the question Mr Bailey had posed about the potential for the witch-hunt-style online and local press reporting to sway a jury. The trial had happened two cities away in order to try to find unbiased people, but how could anyone have avoided reading this stuff? As I thought back to the intense discussions I'd shared with classmates about it all, it seemed surreal that several months later I was sitting right in the middle of the village where it had all unfolded.

Mum's warning tone and words from last night distracted me as I picked through the stories. I tried to shake off the feeling of unease creeping through me at the thought of Mum ever realising it wasn't such a weird co-incidence we had ended up in Christian's village. Dad had encouraged Mum to consider a 'well-to-do place', and immediately Rowantree had flashed in my head, a thrill of excitement at the thought of being able to walk the streets Christian had walked, actually get to know young people who had been at the party that night.

My parents thought it was strange when they both started to receive email alerts from estate agents for property in Rowantree. Mum blamed Dad for adding her to too many lists, telling him to stay out of it, that he'd agreed to let her have the final decision where to go, even if he was paying. Dad blamed her, saying she must have forgotten what she'd signed up for. Neither of them ever realised I had signed them both up.

It was Dad who noticed the flat first, who encouraged us to view it when I said I loved the look of it. I then started to tell Mum how much I wanted to live in the country, to get away from the noise of a town centre. Rowantree was a perfect balance as it was still well connected, with direct trains and buses into town, meaning I didn't need to rely on lifts from Mum.

I chewed on my lip, not quite believing I could be so manipulative. Maybe Mum was right and I had become a bit too obsessed. But seeing Daniel so convinced of his friend's innocence sparked off a new level of curiosity.

A familiar photograph caught my eye – it had accompanied a transcribed podcast where students talked about Patrick and Louise; the perfect happy couple. That debate had appeared not long after whispers of suspicion began to surround Patrick; reports of him drinking too much the night of the party, how he could get jealous and angry when drunk. Anonymous postings started to defend an alternative story: that Christian was not the last person to see Louise alive – that Patrick had entered her parents' bedroom, found them dancing together and launched himself at Christian. Louise had tried to separate them, attempting to calm Patrick down, only firing his rage more. Comments suggested Patrick was dangerously unstable and a controlling boyfriend.

But no witnesses came forward to the police with official statements, all hiding behind anonymous postings online. No one seemed certain enough to place Patrick at the scene of the crime. This particular podcast, started by girls who had now left school, painted such a flattering picture of him; a charming, good-looking boy from a wealthy and well-respected family – his dad a top surgeon, his mum a teacher at the local primary school. Patrick was headed for good things and had been very much in love with Louise; it made no sense that he would end her life. The podcast featured soundbites from press interviews where Mr Marshall shut down any suggestion that Patrick could be involved in his daughter's murder, talking about the closeness of the families, the devastation they all felt.

The locals found it much easier to point the finger of blame towards the weird loner boy who was always in trouble for talking back to teachers, who got caught smoking more than cigarettes behind the sheds at school and who once smashed his bike into the side of Mrs Marshall's new BMW after drinking half a bottle of whisky swiped during a family quiz night at the local pub.

"Darcy!"

My head darted up at Mum's shout. "What?" I

gathered up the stories, shoving them back into my folder.

"Your school bus just left."

I jumped up, glancing at my bedside clock. Eight thirty-five. "Shhh...ugar." I grabbed my bag and stomped into the living room. Mum was casually perched on the arm of the sofa, peering out the window.

"Why didn't you tell me the time?" I grumbled.

"Who am I, your *mother*?" She stuck her tongue out at me.

"And I bet you left me no toast."

"No, but there's jam..."

I pulled my jacket on. "You'll need to give me a lift again today." We'd agreed on my first day I'd skip the village bus ride, but now I'd met a couple of locals I was annoyed to miss it.

"Oh, I see. So then *I*'m late again? How does that work?"

"You're always late anyway. Come on, pleeeeease. It's not going to look good me turning up late on my second day of school. The teachers seem overly concerned about rules in that place."

"Fine, fine. Let's go." Mum jumped up, ruffling my hair on the way past.

We clambered into Wanda and I turned the radio up, the stories about Christian still racing through my head. He had been taken to trial on fairly flimsy evidence: his fingerprints were found on the murder weapon (which had been part of his pirate Halloween costume), and some DNA evidence and scratches on his arm – all of which Christian had an explanation for. Why hadn't his solicitor fought harder for him? Why hadn't *he* fought harder?

"What were you doing all that time in your room

43

anyway?" Mum asked.

"Nothing. I was just taking my time getting ready," I answered nonchalantly. *Just reading up on stories about our local murderer. The one you told me to stop obsessing about.*

My phone beeped in my pocket. I pulled it out, a message from Daniel flashing up.

Sick of us all already? Please tell me you've not escaped back to your old school.

I smiled.

"Is that from your new boyfriend?" Mum shot me another curious glance.

"I don't have a boyfriend. Just a friend *who is a boy.*"

"I see. You exchanged numbers quickly."

I rolled my eyes. "Don't you know my generation have problems talking to one another? We need texts and social media to communicate."

"I thought you deleted your social media accounts."

"Temporarily suspended." Until I worked out the dilemma of how to delete my old life before starting my new one without greatly offending anyone. I wanted to keep in touch with Fee, even although we only messaged occasionally. The evil Jo had no doubt enlisted her into her gang now that I was out of the picture.

"Here we are, mother Lily saves the day!" Mum trilled as she zoomed round the corner into the school car park, nearly crashing into the back of a white Mini.

The seat belt cut into my shoulder as she slammed

on the brakes.

"Jeezus. Why is he going so slow?" Mum smoothed stray curls back from her forehead, swallowing too hard.

A silver-haired head leaned out of the driver's window, turning to shout something indecipherable at us.

"What's he saying?" Mum frowned, switching off the radio, winding her window down. "I can't hear you!" she shouted back.

"Oh my god." I sank lower into my seat as I realised the driver was Mr Harris.

"Mum, wind up your window. Shuttup and wind up your window," I pleaded through gritted teeth.

She swung into a parking space alongside him.

"Mum..." I tried to get her attention, but she was undoing her seatbelt and peering over at his car.

He got out and she reached for the handle of her door.

"What're you doing?" I grabbed her arm. "That's my bloody Art teacher. Don't you *dare* embarrass me."

"Your Art teacher?" she barely acknowledged before stepping out the car.

I turned my head in the opposite direction.

"You nearly took the back of my car off..." Mr Harris started. His words died away when Mum cut in with a cheery hello.

"I'm Darcy's mother. So sorry about the near accident but she missed her bus this morning and I was desperate to get her here on time. Couldn't have her creating a bad impression on her first week."

She'd put on her posh, rational voice. A surge of relief flowed through me that she'd chosen this tactic and not the road rage '*What the hell do you think you're doing?*' approach she was so fond of taking.

"Darcy's mother..." The surprise defused his anger.

I climbed out the car, flashing him a sheepish smile. "Sorry, Mr Harris. My mum's a bit of an overenthusiastic driver."

He scratched his head, turning back to observe Mum. "Not to worry."

They were smiling at each other. I stepped forward, looking between them.

"It's nice to meet you." Mum stuck out her hand and he shook it, their eyes locking.

I frowned. "I should really get to class. Mum, you're going to be late for work..."

"Oh right." She blinked, pulling her hand away, fumbling with the handle. "Have to dash." The bell rang, as if on cue. "There's your bell, don't want to keep you..."

I shot her a curious glance. This was new; a rambling, nervy Mum.

"Have a good day, Darcy. I'll make dinner tonight. Goodbye, Mr Harris." She pulled the door shut, revving up the engine.

I looked at her blankly, wanting to ask when she had ever made dinner.

"It's Timothy." He bent down to the window. "Goodbye, Darcy's mum."

Wanda, the ever-temperamental car, gave a violent surge backwards, almost knocking Mr Harris off his feet. I turned away, unable to watch.

"Sorry!" Mum shouted out the window, the gears crunching as she backed out of the car park.

Mr Harris laughed as she screeched into the distance.

"Sorry." I shook my head. "She's a nightmare."

"Not at all, she's charming." He walked alongside me, still chuckling to himself. "Must keep your dad on his toes?"

"No." I shook my head, taken aback by his blunt question. "I mean, he's not here anymore...he's in London. Better get to class," I mumbled, hurrying up the stairs. Once at the top I turned to look over my shoulder. The smile was still on his lips; a dreamy, far away kind of smile that made him appear too young and un-teacher-like. It was disconcerting.

Chapter Five

"You're here."

Hands grabbed the straps of my bag, pulling me backwards. I turned to see Daniel smiling at me.

"Of course," I said, falling into step with him. "Didn't feel like slumming it on the bus today so got my chauffeur to drop me off."

"I see." He nodded.

We walked in silence up the stairs to our first class.

"You know how you said Mr Harris and Christian's mum...had a thing? Are they still seeing each other?"

He stopped walking. "Why d'you ask?"

"No reason really. Just a weird moment in the car park earlier."

He looked a bit alarmed. "What like?" His eyes narrowed. "Like a weird moment between you and Mr Harris?"

"No!" I held up my hands, shaking my head frantically. *Why would he ask that?* "God no. Mum nearly crashed into his car and then they said hello, got a bit gooey-eyed."

"Oh." He resumed walking. "I think when she moved away they stopped seeing each other. I don't really know what happened. It's not exactly top of the list of things me and Christian chat about."

"No, of course," I said quickly. "So, have you heard from Christian lately?" I asked casually.

Daniel shrugged. "I emailed him the other day. Today's Tuesday...so I think he can make a call this evening. I asked him to call me so we could have a proper chat."

"D'you think it would be okay if *I* emailed him?" The words were out before I had time to think them through.

Daniel stopped again, nearly sending a first-year flying. I reached out to steady the girl, who clutched her bag closer, like she thought I might mug her. She cast nervous looks over her shoulder on her way down the corridor.

I realised Daniel was studying me intently. I raised an eyebrow in question.

"Why would you want to email him?" he said.

Why did I want to email him? Curiosity? So that I could tell him not everyone believed he was a crazed murderer? "I'm not sure."

"You're not sure..." Daniel said slowly, his frown deepening.

"Maybe because I think he could do with another friend? And if you guys are friends and I'm your new friend then it kind of makes it less weird."

"Me and you are friends?"

I searched his eyes, becoming more unnerved the longer he just stood there, still frowning. I started to feel stupid, my face flushing. "I thought you'd said yesterday, just before you shook my hand...?"

His face broke into a cheeky grin. "Of course. I'm just teasing." He slapped me on the shoulder. "I think I should run it by him first. If you want to email I have to give you his prisoner number and he'd really need to give me the okay for that. If he does call tonight, I'll ask him."

"Okay." I nodded. "That sounds like a good idea. D'you think he'll think I'm weird wanting to email?"

"Probably," Daniel said casually, walking into our class.

"Great," I said, following him in.

*

"Darcy, your phone just beeped," Mum called from the living room.

I laid down the folder of articles that I'd returned to reading after we'd finished dinner and hurried into the living room.

My heart lurched as I read the message from Daniel.

He said it's okay for you to contact him.

The rest contained Christian's prisoner number and instructions of how to access the prisoner email account online.

"Who's it from?" Mum asked, glancing up from her magazine.

"Fee," I lied, re-reading the message, grabbing my netbook and heading back through to my bedroom.

"How is she?" Mum called.

"Fine!" I shouted back, shutting my door over. I fired up my browser and typed in the web address for 'Email a prisoner'. I clicked into the *How it Works* and *FAQ sections*, scanning through the registration instructions. Daniel had already explained that I'd be able to email Christian but he couldn't email me back. I scanned the information – the emails got printed off and delivered to prisoners' cells by staff. The offenders' unit would also charge me forty pence an email, which seemed a pointless amount. I looked out my bank card and began the sign-in process.

And then I was ready to begin the email. I sat back on my bed, leaning against the wall. What on earth could I type that wouldn't sound pathetic?

Hi Christian, How are you? It totally sucks that you've been put in a young offenders' unit. I bet the food tastes awful...

My toes curled as I read it back and I frantically pressed down on the delete button.

A photo of him was lying on the floor, looking up at me. One that was in colour, published to accompany a detailed story in the midst of his trial. He was wearing a Smashing Pumpkins t-shirt. I'd never noticed that before. The hairs on my arm stood up. That *had* to be a positive sign, that I should email him, that this wasn't a totally insane idea.

Dear Christian,

My name's Darcy (named after the bass player from the Smashing Pumpkins, minus the apostrophe. If I was a boy I was going to be Billy. I'm glad I'm a girl).

So Daniel has probably already filled you in a bit about me (maybe?). I've just moved to Rowantree with Mum (my parents recently separated) and I started at Finlay Academy. So far it's been okay – Daniel is helping me to settle in and I have to say I'm glad he's around as Kara and her friends are a bit intimidating.

I paused at that bit. Should I even mention Kara? It would make him think of Patrick and he would be the last person Christian would want to be reminded of. My finger hovered over the delete button. No, I'd keep it for now.

Mum and me moved into the swanky flats on Kyle Road. It's Dad's way of trying to buy our forgiveness but he's going to have to work a lot harder than this. Mum has forgiven him way too easily and that makes me more mad - that she just let him disappear down to London without even giving him a hard time. Sorry, you don't even know me and here I am attempting to tell you my life story.

So I guess you're wondering why I'm writing to you. I have to be honest, I'm not really sure myself. I suppose I think it must be awful for you, getting sent to a young offenders' unit. I can't even begin to imagine what life in there must be like for you. If I was stuck somewhere like hell I guess I'd appreciate it if someone attempted to communicate with me from the outside world. So that's what I'm offering – a hello from out here, an attempt at friendship maybe? If you're Daniel's friend you've got to be alright.

I paused, contemplating finishing with an 'oh and by the way I think you're innocent', but decided it might sound a bit cheesy or insincere. Instead I signed off with a simple 'hope to hear from you soon', typing my postal address under my name so he could write me a letter back. Mum would freak at that.

After re-reading the email five times I held my breath and clicked send, my words released into cyber space, hurtling towards Christian Henderson.

Chapter Six

I munched on my cereal, watching with amusement as Mum pouted in the mirror, dabbing at her siren-red lips.

"Looking hot." I grabbed my bag from under her feet and slung it over my shoulder.

"Where you going?" She grabbed her handbag, fluffing her hair, coming up behind me.

"School. Where are you going? A disco?"

"Very funny." She made a face. "I thought I'd give you a lift again."

"That's okay. I'm early today, plenty of time to walk down for my bus," I said, opening the door.

"Oh, but it's no trouble. And you can't trust bus drivers these days."

I turned to face her. "I want to get the bus today, Mum. I need to fit in and that's not going to happen if Kara catches on that I'm getting a lift from you every day."

Her face fell. "You're right. You should slum it with the rest of them."

"But don't worry, I'll do some investigating for you..."

"What d'you mean?" She attempted to look innocent.

I smiled. "About Mr Harris's status and hangouts. So you can stalk him by other means."

"I have no idea what you're talking about..." She smiled ruefully, suddenly finding the contents of her handbag interesting. "Be off with you, daughter."

"Have a good day." I waved, skipping down the stairs. As I turned the corner to the ground floor, a door opened and Kara walked out. Our eyes met.

"Hi." I smiled tentatively.

She nodded in acknowledgement, slamming the door shut behind her. I tried not to stare at her short skirt and legs that went on for miles. Even in nine inch heels my legs could never look like that.

I hesitated, waiting for her to fall into step beside me. "Your gran's a really great cook – we enjoyed her casserole. I'll bring the dish back later."

Kara shrugged. "Okay."

I clammed up, wondering if I should just walk on.

Kara sighed, as if sensing my thoughts. "Look, I know I've been a bit off. Zoe and Patrick were saying I should probably give you a break."

I blinked in surprise.

"I'm not saying we're going to be best mates or anything, but we're all going to Patrick's house next Saturday night for my birthday if you want to come over?"

Had I actually heard that right? "Um, sure, great."

"You can bring your boyfriend if you want."

It took me another bemused minute to figure out she meant Daniel. "Oh, Daniel isn't…"

Kara didn't let me finish, hurrying ahead as Patrick came into view at the bus stop. He pulled her into a hug, kissing her on the neck.

"Hi, Darcy." He waved at me over her shoulder and I waved back, watching as Kara's grip on him tightened.

"Hey, dude."

I turned to see Daniel. "Hey."

"So, we get the honour of your presence today."

"Yeah my chauffeur has some important celeb to ferry about this morning."

I pulled at his arm, so he didn't walk too close to

Kara and Patrick. "The weirdest thing just happened...Kara invited me to one of their social gatherings next weekend."

Daniel made a face.

"I think you're invited too," I said.

"Great," he mumbled. "So, Christian had a lot of questions about you when I spoke to him on the phone," he said, changing the subject.

"Oh, yeah?" I tried not to sound too interested.

"He was curious why some girl he doesn't know wants to email him."

I blushed. That probably meant he thought I was a weirdo. "I sent him an email last night, actually."

"That was quick. I guess he'll get his answer soon, then."

"What did you say about me?"

Daniel smirked. "I told him you're totally nuts. Have an obsession with criminals. That you wear a 'Free Christian' t-shirt to bed."

"Nice, thanks." What if he really did think I was nuts? What if I actually *was*? People wrote articles about women writing to men on death row, like it was some sort of psychological mystery. But Christian wasn't on death row, I told myself. And now I was friends with one of his friends it gave me more of a connection.

"Relax, I told him you're cool and that you're on his side. But don't be offended if he's a bit abrupt with you to start with; that's if he even responds...he's a bit wary of everyone these days."

A surge of disappointment hit as we boarded the bus. I'd naively never entertained the possibility that he might not reply.

*

A week passed. No letter arrived. Maybe Daniel

was right and Christian wasn't going to respond.

*

"Heard from Christian lately?" I tried to keep the question casual as I joined Daniel at the sink in Art class, washing paint brushes. It was nine days since I'd sent the email.

"Still no response, huh? He's not replied to one of my emails either. It might just mean he's having a bad couple of weeks."

"Oh." I tried to imagine what a 'bad' time would be like in there. "Does he have a lot of bad weeks?"

"Think of all the worst guys you've ever encountered in school. Then imagine living with them in a confined space on a daily basis." Daniel's face clouded over. "I don't think he ever has a good week to be honest."

"Does he have to share a cell – is that even the right word – with a lot of boys?"

"Just the one. I think he's okay, the guy. He is now, anyway. Christian's smart. He can figure people out quickly and I think that worked to his advantage this time because he won Sean over. Impressed him with his art work."

"Excuse me."

The voice behind us made me jump. I moved aside to let Zoe into the sink to dump her brushes.

"Nice work, Darcy."

I turned to see Mr Harris standing at my desk, studying my painting.

"Thanks."

"She's a genius, that girl," Patrick said, winking at me. He was back in his old seat, beside Zoe, but still paid me too much attention.

"Maybe some of that genius will rub off on you one day, Mr Barrington," Mr Harris said dryly.

The bell rang and I stacked up the paints. I was aware that Mr Harris was still hovering at my desk.

He waited for the table next to me to clear and glanced around, as if checking no one else was watching, then slid a flyer under my painting. "I've got an exhibition coming up this weekend. Thought you and your mum might want to come along to the opening night. Daniel is welcome to come along too."

"Oh, okay." I nodded, face burning, grabbing the flyer without looking. At least now Mum might stop prancing around like a demented cat, asking me unsubtle questions about my Art classes. But what if they actually started going out? I watched as Mr Harris walked around the room, picking up discarded paint brushes. What if he started hanging around our flat, having dinner with us and stuff. I shuddered. I'd have to drop out of Art if it all went wrong... Mum wasn't even officially divorced yet.

"What's that?" Daniel grabbed the flyer out my hand.

"Mr Harris invited me to his exhibition."

"Teacher's Pet."

"I don't think it's me he wants to pet," I mumbled, nearly making myself gag at the thought. "The invite's really for my mum – I'm just the decoy. He said you could come too...and you will, right?"

"Free wine," Daniel read. "I'll be there. Hey, isn't Saturday night Kara and Patrick's *social gathering*?"

I grabbed the flyer, looking at the times. "This starts at six...we can head over to Patrick's afterwards."

"We?" Daniel made a face. "There's no way I'm going to that asswipe's house."

I followed Daniel down the corridor, already hatching a plan of persuasion. There was no way I could handle turning up at the party without him.

*

The letter was the first thing I saw when I opened the door. My name was clearly printed in black ink, an HM stamp in the corner. My heart thumped as I grabbed it from the mat, studying the handwriting. Neat, blunt and kind of artistic.

Hands shaking, I ripped open the envelope and unfolded the paper. I held my breath as I read the contents.

Dear Darcy,

Thanks for your letter. I'm not really sure what to say in response. I find it confusing when girls I don't even know have the desire to write to me – a convicted murderer. You do realise I was convicted of stabbing my female classmate?

My whole body cringed. Now I just felt stupid.

So, you can maybe understand it makes me wonder about you... what drives you to want to connect with me. Some of the girls who write to me profess my innocence. Say I was wronged. Maybe that's what you believe? Others call Louise all sorts of nasty names, like it was *her* fault that she got stabbed. Really, you can't imagine some of the disturbing, stupid mail I receive in here.

I know you attempted to give an explanation for your email, that because I'm Daniel's friend you've decided I'm ok and think we could maybe be friends. So I guess I'm relying on Daniel's judgement here too (he said you're alright).

He sounded almost happy, for the first time in a long while, when I spoke to him on the phone last week. That's important. I like the idea that you're there, being his friend. So don't turn out to be like the rest of them, okay?

I smiled.

This is a short one for now.
I'm curious to receive more emails from you though. Maybe because I like your name.
Later,
Christian Henderson

Hands properly shaking, I sat down on the sofa, re-reading the letter, skimming past the opening bit. I couldn't believe I was actually reading words that Christian himself had written. After spending so long wondering what he was really like, having to piece together a picture of him from others' opinions, it felt surreal communicating directly. I paced the room, feeling a mix of excitement and anxiety. Daniel had warned me lots of girls sent Christian letters, but I hadn't stopped to think what they would write about. The last bit helped settle my embarrassment and was a reassurance that it was okay for me to keep emailing him.

The most important thing would be to keep it casual, make sure he understood one hundred per cent that I wasn't a weird stalker. I swallowed, glancing at the envelope with my address on it. Was I being stupid, allowing him into my life?

As I heard Mum's key rattling in the lock I slid the letter carefully into my bag, the sentences now locked in my head. The words 'a convicted murderer' flashed to the forefront.

The fact he'd actually referred to himself as a murderer was strange, when he'd always professed his innocence. Did it mean he had totally given up, or was it a test, to find out if I was brave enough to face the possibility that he could be?

The Party: Scene Three

Pain, like needles, stabbed at his arm as Christian ran along the hallway. He rolled up his sleeve, dabbing at the blood pooling at the wounds. Her nails had been like talons, slicing at his skin.

As he hurried along the hallway, he collided with a small brunette dressed as a zombie bride. They looked at one another, each taking a few minutes to register who hid beneath the costume.

Then she noticed the blood.

"Christian, your arm. Are you okay?" Zoe reached out to touch him. He recoiled, startling her.

"Don't touch me; I'm fine."

Anger was pumping through his body, Patrick and Louise's words still raw.

"Nothing's going on, I swear, Patrick. As if I'd be interested in that freak. He was coming on to me."

"Is that right, you creepy loser? Think you can get my girl alone in here and attack her?"

"Patrick, you're drunk...calm down. He didn't mean any harm. We were just dancing."

"Out the way, Lou. He's going to get what he deserves. Coming here, acting like he's something. You're nothing, mate. Everyone knows it. We all think you're a joke. Did you know that?"

Christian punched the wall in anger. Zoe hesitated, placing a hand on his back.

"Are you okay? I was looking for you earlier but couldn't find you."

He closed his eyes, resting his forehead against the wall. The warmth of Zoe's hand on his back was reassuring and he felt the anxiety and anger calm. He turned to talk to her, but when he opened his eyes she had moved further along the hall and was confronting a girl dressed in a zombie nurse outfit, tight white dress and gloves tainted with fake blood.

"What are you doing here? I told you to stay at home and look after Mum. Are you drunk?"

The girl, who he now recognised as Zoe's younger sister, Roo, rolled her eyes. "Mum's sleeping. She took a chill pill, just like you need to. Louise invited me. I think I deserve some fun too."

"Mum will freak. Like she doesn't have enough to worry about. Why can't you stay in and watch cheesy films like other thirteen-year-olds?"

Christian didn't want to stick around to hear more drama and arguments. He shoved past people drinking on the stairs, wanting to escape the house, escape everyone. Music vibrated through the floorboards, bouncing off the walls; girls were screaming, laughing. He needed to find a quiet place and silence his mind. Why did he ever think he could belong here, with them?

"Hey, mate." A glassy-eyed gangster stepped into his path at the front door.

"Out the way." Christian reached past him for the handle.

"Got a light, mate?" The gangster blocked the door, holding up a cigar.

Christian instinctively felt his pockets, pictured the lighter lying upstairs on the bedroom cabinet. He cursed, braced to turn back.

"Woah." The gangster swayed, grabbing at his arm. "Did you feel that? Did the hallway just spin? I think I'm gonna puke..."

Christian grimaced as the boy showered his top with bright blue sick.

"Fantastic. Thank you!"

"Oh, mate, sorry...sorry." The gangster lunged forward, trying to wipe his top.

"Leave it," Christian growled. He pulled the door open, running out into the night, nearly falling over a couple kissing on the front steps. They didn't even look up, the guy pulling her head further towards him.

Christian's feet pounded the pavements as he ran down the hill, ran past dog walkers, his heart crashing in his ears.

It wasn't until he reached his house that he realised tears stung his eyes. He backed against the front door, catching his breath, and wiped at his face. The rancid smell of the vomit on his clothes caused him to gag. He doubled over, breathing in the cold air.

"You okay, son?"

His neighbour, Mr Holt, hesitated at the end of the drive, his dog panting in anticipation.

Christian straightened up, angling his body towards the door so that Mr Holt couldn't see the mess of his top. He didn't want the neighbours thinking he was some stupid drunk. "Fine. Thanks." He gave what he hoped was a reassuring wave.

"Alright, son. Have a good night."

Christian fumbled with his key and fell inside.

Chapter Seven

"What do you wear to an Art Exhibition?" Mum shouted from her bedroom.

"More importantly, what do you wear to a Patrick and Kara party?" I mumbled, frowning at my reflection. "A suit of armour? Or radioactive suit... just in case."

"What're you muttering about?"

I spun round and did a double take at the sophisticated woman standing in my doorway.

"Woah, Mum. You look smokin'."

She blushed, self-consciously smoothing down her dress. "Not too much?"

"No, it's perfect. Casual enough to look like you've just chucked it on; sexy enough to make Mr Harris sweat." I frowned. "Actually, scrap that last bit. Horrible images are now flashing through my head."

Mum joined me at the mirror, running a hand gently down my hair. She locked eyes with me, her expression serious. "Is this too weird for you, Darcy? Socialising with your teacher?"

I hesitated. "A bit. But it's okay; he seems cool and almost human for a teacher. You deserve some fun...just not too much fun." I tried to wink but it turned into a twitch and she laughed.

"You look really pretty in that dress." Mum smiled at me in the mirror and I viewed my reflection critically. A black skater dress with a camel belt and camel heels. That was about as sophisticated as I'd ever get.

"It shows off my knobbly knees."

"Girls would kill to have those legs," Mum dismissed.

"I hope not," I mumbled. Her choice of phrase did nothing to ease my nerves about going to a party at Patrick Barrington's house.

"I'm still not sure about you going to that party afterwards, Darcy," Mum frowned, almost like she could read my mind.

"It'll be fine. Daniel will look after me. Once you meet him you'll be reassured that he will be a great bodyguard. He must be like six two at least."

"Nice." Mum winked and I pulled a face.

"None of that. Please." I shot her a warning look.

"I'll be on my best behaviour. Promise," she grinned and threw my coat at me. "Come on, let's hit the town."

*

"So she peed herself the first day of Nursery? And threw up over her teacher the first day of Primary?" Daniel guffawed in the back. "Did I miss something spectacular your first day at our school, Darcy?"

"No," I said, shooting Mum death glares. "I now have full control of my bodily functions, thank you."

Mum and Daniel laughed and I looked out the window, sulking.

"Any more good stories, Mrs..."

"Lily," Mum cut in, glancing at Daniel through the mirror. "Hmm, let me see..."

"Mum, he's heard enough. I think we're here anyway." I squinted out the window, recognising the white shop front from the gallery website. Fairy lights were strung along the windows, a crowd already gathered inside.

"I hope there's no other teachers here," Daniel said as Mum manoeuvred into a space further up the street.

"Or pupils," I added.

"Kids, kids, where's your school spirit?" Mum chided as she fought with the steering wheel, trying to get Wanda to fit into the space.

Ten minutes later the three of us were standing outside the gallery, hovering nervously at the door.

Mum looked a bit sick.

"You okay?" I whispered, squeezing her arm.

"No. It looks like there's a bunch of really arty intellectuals in there. What am I going to say to them?"

"Talk to them about books. You're a librarian; you can out-intellectualise any one of them."

"Out-intellectualise? I don't think that's even a word," Daniel said.

"It's not. I like to make up words when I can't think of something that fits my sentence." I shrugged, pushing the door open.

Immediately I sensed a chilled vibe to the place; the subdued conversation punctuated with jazzy beats from a stereo in the corner as people stood drinking wine, or wandered slowly between paintings. My eyes were drawn to the brighter canvasses; bleeding sunsets and lavender fields. Mr Harris could paint. I was impressed.

"Holy crap. There's a naked woman at that back wall," Daniel hissed in my ear.

"What?" I turned round in horror, expecting to see an actual naked woman sprawled up against the back wall but relaxed when I realised it was a sketch; quite a beautiful, classy nude sketch. "That's called life drawing, Daniel."

"Cool," Daniel grinned. "Can't wait till we get onto that in class."

I rolled my eyes just as Mr Harris appeared by our side.

"So glad you could all make it." Mr Harris shook our hands heartily, all the time smiling at Mum, his handshake with her lasting a bit too long. "Hello again, Darcy's mum."

"Call me Lily." Mum blushed, and my toes curled a bit in my shoes.

"Gladly, Lily. That's a beautiful name." He smiled and I shot Daniel an alarmed look.

He smirked, mouthing, '*He's got it baaad.*'

I subtly kicked him on the back of his leg and he lunged forward. Mum frowned at us and I smiled sweetly.

"Your work's really beautiful," Mum said, gesturing towards the paintings.

"Thank you. Let me get you a drink." Mr Harris nodded towards a table at the door.

"Just a soft drink is fine. I'm driving," she said, following him towards the table.

Mr Harris turned to us.

"We're fine." I waved a hand. "Just going to have a proper look at your work." I grabbed Daniel and pulled him in the opposite direction. "We should give them some alone time."

"Doesn't it freak you out?" Daniel said.

"What?"

"Mr Harris flirting with your mum."

I shrugged. "She seems to like him. She deserves some attention."

"Just make sure Kara doesn't hear about it – she'd make your life hell."

That was the last thing I wanted now that Kara was being almost civilised at school.

"Speaking of Kara..." I smiled up at him,

fluttering my eyelashes.

"What?" Daniel folded his arms. "Why are you doing that funny thing with your eyes?"

"The party..."

"The one I'm not going to," Daniel said.

"Thing is, Mum will only let me go if you come with me. So you can look after me."

He snorted. "What are you, like, ten?"

"Please, Daniel." I touched him on the arm. "I feel like I have to go. It might make Kara friendlier in the long run. I don't want to become their best friends or anything, just make life a bit more bearable at school. You know?"

A shadow fell across Daniel's face. "Yeah, I know. I once thought like that – go along to their stupid parties and try to fit in and maybe they'll start to like you."

My body tensed.

"But the last party I went to didn't exactly go like that."

"I know," I mumbled. "I get why you don't really want to go...but what if we can find out things, by hanging around with them."

"Find out things?" Daniel frowned. "What d'you think's going to happen? You get Patrick drunk and extract some big confession? You don't think I've tried that?"

"Well, have you?" I asked quietly.

"Trust me, I've tried." Daniel rolled up his shirt sleeve to reveal a small red mark on his arm.

"What's that?" I frowned, reaching out to touch it.

Daniel pulled back, letting the sleeve drop. "Patrick burnt my arm with his cigarette. He says it was an accident, but it was in the middle of a heated conversation I had with him about his whereabouts the night of that party. The wheels of my BMX were also slashed that day."

"Are you serious?" A rage rose inside me, but also alarm. Surely Patrick reacting like that was a major indication of his guilt, clearly not wanting anyone probing too deep to reveal the truth.

Daniel's mouth set in a grim line. "Still want to go to their stupid party?"

Conflicting emotions shot through my body – a big part of me wanted to just keep out of their way, hide in the shadows with Daniel. But then an image of Christian flashed through my head, his lost expression in those press pictures, like the whole world had abandoned him.

"I have to," I said, determined. "Are you going to let me go alone?" I pleaded with him silently. I knew when it came to it I wouldn't have the courage to go without him.

Daniel let out a long sigh and peered at me through narrowed eyes. "You're really annoying, you know?"

"Does that mean you'll come?" I grinned.

"I suppose. But just for a couple of hours, okay?"

"Deal." I held out my hand for Daniel to shake but he was looking over my shoulder, surprise and confusion on his face.

"What is it?" I followed his gaze and saw an attractive petite woman standing between Mum and Mr Harris. Her hair was a mass of brown curls and I could tell from the way her arm gesticulated a bit too wildly, and the way her wine was sloshing up at the sides of her glass, that she was quite drunk. Mr Harris's face was ashen and bent close to hers, like he was speaking quietly, trying to calm her. Mum looked stricken.

"Who's she?" I asked, just as I began to process the sharp features, the striking blue eyes.

Daniel shook his head slightly, like he couldn't quite believe what he was seeing. "It's Christian's mum."

Chapter Eight

"What's she doing here?" I watched as Mr Harris manoeuvred Mrs Henderson to one side, leaving Mum sipping nervously on her orange juice, her cheeks flushed. "You said she and Mr Harris were finished."

Daniel shrugged. "I thought they were."

"Mum looks mortified. Come on, let's go and save her."

People were casting curious glances in Mrs Henderson's direction as her voice grew louder and more animated. I caught the phrase, "...already...it didn't take you long, Timothy."

"You okay?" I snuck in beside Mum.

"I really wish I'd left the car at home, so I could down that bottle of wine," Mum answered, eyeing up the Shiraz.

"What was she saying?" I asked, nodding towards Mrs Henderson.

"Her exact words were: *Good evening, Timothy...bet you weren't expecting to see me here. Saw you had an exhibition on and couldn't resist coming along, seeing as you never returned my phone calls or replied to my emails... Oh hello, you must be Timothy's new LOVER.*" Mum sucked in her breath.

I covered my face with my hand, hoping Mum had got carried away with her impression.

"I think I want to leave now." Mum put her glass down on the table and slid her coat back on.

"No, wait." Daniel held up his hand to get our attention. "It's okay, Mrs... Lily. I think Mrs Henderson's just had a bit too much to drink. She's okay, really."

"Mrs Henderson? You know her?" Mum looked at Daniel in surprise. "Is she one of your teachers?" Mum looked to me for answers.

I shook my head. "It's Christian Henderson's mum."

"Christian...that boy...the murderer?"

I flinched.

"He's not a murderer," Daniel said, his eyes flashing.

Mum's face softened. "I'm sorry, Daniel. Darcy told me you and Christian were friends."

"*Are* friends. He's still my best friend," Daniel said.

"Daniel! Is that you?"

Christian's mum moved past Mr Harris, hurrying towards Daniel, a smile spreading across her face.

"Look at you." She pulled him towards her in a hug, reaching up to ruffle his hair. "So tall and handsome. You look like you've grown about a foot since I last saw you."

Daniel smiled. "Hi, Mrs Henderson. How are you?"

"Oh, you know." She smiled forlornly, her eyes heavy with too much sadness.

A look of sympathy flashed across Mum's face.

"So, who's your friend?" Mrs Henderson smiled at me and I flushed, almost feeling like I was in the presence of a celebrity, which was ridiculous.

"This is Darcy." Daniel turned to me. "She just moved to Rowantree."

"And I'm Darcy's mum, Lily. I don't think we were properly introduced." Mum stepped forward, holding out her hand.

Mrs Henderson hesitated. I thought for a minute

she was going to ignore Mum, but then she relented and shook her hand. "Julia Henderson. You've maybe heard of my boy, Christian."

"Yes," Mum nodded. "I'm sorry."

"I don't need your sympathy." Julia's eyes were defiant.

Mr Harris appeared, clearing his throat. "All okay here?"

"Fine, Timothy," Julia said dryly. "I'm not going to cause a scene if that's what you're worried about."

Mr Harris shifted uncomfortably, shooting Mum apologetic looks.

"So, how's life in...Oakbridge?" Daniel cut in, clearly trying to lighten the mood.

"It's good, Daniel. Just the change of scene I needed and it makes it a bit easier to visit Christian. I've got decent neighbours too."

"Have you seen Christian lately? How's he doing?"

"Okay, son. It's hard, but he's doing okay." Julia nodded, choosing not to answer the first part of the question.

I wondered if Christian discouraged visits from her, as he did with Daniel. That would be difficult. Or maybe a relief. I tried to imagine how she must feel – what it must be like having to walk away each time, not being able to take her son home.

"And he really appreciates your support." She smiled tightly, squeezing Daniel's arm.

"Of course," Daniel said.

"And how are you liking Rowantree, Darcy?" Julia turned to me.

"It's fine so far, thanks," I said, surprised that she was paying me attention.

"I'm sure Daniel will appreciate a friend at Finlay

Academy," she said.

"Gee, thanks, make me sound like a loser," Daniel joked.

"Not at all, son. That's the label I'd attach to the other locals."

"Well, the other kids have invited them to a party tonight, actually," Mum cut in.

Oh, good one, Mum. I widened my eyes, trying to signal to her to stop talking.

Mr Harris looked at Daniel in surprise. "Where's the party?"

Daniel met my eye and we didn't say anything, knowing what kind of reaction it would provoke from Christian's mum.

"What's his name, Darcy?" Mum prompted. I shook my head violently, willing Mum to pick up on my cues. "Paul? No, Patrick..."

"Patrick Barrington?" Julia's eyes flashed. "Daniel? You're going to his party?"

"Why not?" Mum started to say, baffled. Mr Harris took her arm, manoeuvring her away.

"Why don't we go and have a wander, Lily? There's some people I was hoping to introduce you to this evening."

Mum hesitated and I nodded my head, urging her to go.

I waited until they'd left then started to explain, so Daniel didn't have to. "I'm making Daniel come along, Mrs Henderson. Kara invited me and I thought I'd better go... She's not exactly been very welcoming and I thought I should make the effort."

Julia made a face. "I can imagine. Stuck up princess that she is. Why d'you want to go then, love?"

"Exactly what I've been saying," Daniel said,

folding his arms.

I hesitated, wondering how honest I should be with her. Maybe I'd upset her if I tried to explain my thoughts on Christian. "I'm curious to get to know them better. Maybe in the hope of discovering some truth about that night..."

She really looked at me now, her eyes narrowing. "What d'you mean, Darcy?"

I glanced at Daniel, checking for signs I should shut up, but he looked like he wanted me to continue.

I explained how I had followed Christian's trial online, and that it bothered me the way he was portrayed; and that a lot of the evidence seemed circumstantial, not concrete. I was conscious I was talking too fast, but I kept going, scared to even look at Mrs Henderson in case she was annoyed, or thought I was weird.

"It doesn't seem right, that someone can be convicted on what appears to be character assassination. What if there's more to the story? What if we" - I gestured to Daniel - "could find out the truth?"

"Infiltrate the inner circle?" Julia said quietly.

I couldn't quite read her expression. "Well, yeah," I said, hoping I didn't sound completely stupid.

"Like I tried to, sort of," Daniel said, looking almost apologetic. "I guess I didn't really make a proper go of it. I have anger issues with them."

Julia touched his hand, shaking her head slightly, like she was telling him it was okay.

She laid a hand on my shoulder, her expression serious. "Just be careful, Darcy. They're a tight inner circle in that village, those kids. They won't like you poking your nose into their business."

I swallowed, wondering if I was up for the task.

Then I looked into her eyes properly, saw the haunted expression that matched Christian's in the photos I'd seen. It sent a chill through me and fired a new anger. If someone had let an innocent boy be consumed by the system then this was a truth worth fighting for.

*

The bus on the way back to Rowantree smelled like chips and wet dogs. Daniel steamed up the window, drawing funny faces and writing words backwards.

"That was an intense evening." I puffed a sigh of relief that we had escaped. "Hope Mum didn't mind me abandoning her."

"She'll be fine. She has *Timothy* to look after her." Daniel snorted.

I punched him on the arm.

"Ow." He rubbed his shoulder. "You hit hard for a girl. That might come in handy if Patrick comes anywhere near you later."

I shuddered. "He'll be too busy sticking his tongue down Kara's throat." I chewed on my nails, realising that, thanks to my anti-social tendencies, it was the first proper party I'd been to. I wasn't sure what to expect. Panic fluttered in my chest. And what if Daniel abandoned me as soon as we walked in the door? "Can you promise me something?"

He looked at me expectantly.

"Let's not drink any alcohol. I want to keep my wits about me and I couldn't face dealing with a drunk you."

"Wasn't planning on touching a drop. Patrick looks the type to raid his parents' spirits cabinet and I'm strictly a beer man myself." Daniel puffed up his chest and I rolled my eyes, suspecting his alcohol consumption probably amounted to a sneaky half can on special occasions, like Hogmanay, under parental supervision.

I played about with my phone, looking up when I realised Daniel was watching me. I shot him a questioning look.

"You really seem to care about Christian and his case. Why is that?"

I hesitated, not really knowing how to explain. "I guess I've watched a lot of documentaries that have disturbed me, where innocent people have gone to jail. It's scary how easy it is for the wrong person to be convicted. And something about his case, it just didn't seem right. Like too many presumptions were made, with not enough facts."

I thought back to the harrowed look in Christian's Mum's eyes. She was alone now, no husband and no son at home. And Christian – how did he feel? Being abandoned by his dad, now by the justice system.

"I can't imagine how it would feel being forgotten about twice," I mumbled.

Daniel frowned. "What do you mean?"

I tried to explain and was mortified when I could feel my eyes welling up when I mentioned Christian's dad leaving him. The emotion caught me off guard. It was so easy to bury it, to put a brave face on everything. I realised I took after Mum like that; present a breezy outward demeanour even if I was crumbling inside.

Daniel laid his hand on mine and embarrassment nearly made me pull away, but it felt surprisingly comforting.

"Do you miss your dad?" he asked gently.

I nodded, chewing hard down on my lip so that I wouldn't cry. He squeezed my hand, then went back to looking out the window and I relaxed, relieved that he didn't expect me to open up any more.

The bus dropped us at the bottom of Hunter Hill and Daniel led the way up a steep path beyond my flat complex, to the mansion-sized houses on Lomond Road.

"Can't you just *smmmmell* the money," Daniel said, poking fun at himself as well as Patrick, as I knew he lived around this area too.

"Is Patrick's house bigger than yours?" I asked in a childish voice.

"Maybe. But he doesn't have a pool table." Daniel grinned.

"You have a pool table? When are you inviting me round to play?"

"Whenever," Daniel shrugged. "But my mum is mega annoying. She'll try to offer you cucumber sandwiches and homemade lemonade, like she's hosting a garden party. It's embarrassing."

"That sounds nice!" I protested. "I don't even think my mum knows what a cucumber is." As we turned the corner I looked up at a whitewashed house with a distinctive balcony winding around the windows at the side. I recognised it instantly from the photographs. "That's Louise's house."

Daniel didn't even look up. "Was."

A shiver ran through me as I tried to block out images of what had happened there. "Sorry, it must be kind of weird having to walk past it every day."

He shrugged. "It's not like the Marshalls are there just now anyway. Another family are there while they're in France."

"Just temporarily?"

"It was up for sale for a while, but no one wanted to buy, so it gets rented out. Can't exactly hide the fact a murder took place there, so I reckon it put people off. And I think they got sick of so many people just coming to view it out of morbid curiosity. Some photos appeared online of the 'scene of the murder' I believe."

I shook my head in disgust. Some people were sick. "I guess Kara was relieved she had the option to live elsewhere."

"Yeah," Daniel said. He turned to walk up a winding driveway and I knew from the loud music and lights shining from every window that we'd reached Patrick's house. It was one of the biggest houses on the street, massive bay windows extending to three floors. Did it come with a tennis court and cinema?

My palms started to sweat as we headed up the drive, heart thumping at the prospect of having to make small talk with a bunch of teenagers I wasn't sure even liked me. A part of me was tempted to turn back - to suggest to Daniel we go to play pool at his instead - but then I thought of Christian and his mum. I imagined if I was locked up for something I didn't do, how panicked and helpless I would feel, and how broken Mum would be.

"Ready for the worst night of your life?" Daniel quipped as he rang the doorbell.

Chapter Nine

My body relaxed a bit when Zoe answered the door.

"Come in." She stepped aside, shooting us curious glances – not in a threatening manner like Kara, more like she was trying to figure us out.

I smiled hello and noted with interest that Zoe looked at Daniel intently on his way past. In true boy style, he remained oblivious to any attention; too busy eyeing up the chess set which was displayed on a large marble table beneath the winding staircase. Maybe he was the reason Zoe had suggested Kara take it easy on me.

As we followed Zoe down the massive hallway, I stared at Daniel's back objectively. He was quite handsome; tall, broad shoulders, a cool rock vibe going on. He probably had a lot of female admirers at school that he was unaware of. I thought back to how nice it had felt on the bus when he gave my hand a reassuring squeeze. I shook the thought away, not wanting to complicate things.

Zoe led us into a kitchen, complete with breakfast bar, that was about triple the size of our living room. I recognised a couple of girls from my Psychology class, sitting on stools, smiling up at some older boys I didn't know. Others stood around leaning on counters, popping ice cubes out of trays, pouring drinks, laughing and dancing to music that blared through digital speakers.

I stayed close to Daniel, practically hiding behind him. I could tell from the way he stood, poker straight, that he was trying to present a confident air, but there was definite fear behind his eyes. It reassured me, that he felt as awkward as me.

"What do you guys want to drink?" Zoe gestured to a row of bottles. I read the labels: vodka, Jack Daniels, peach schnapps, whisky, Tia Maria, some kind of tropical cocktail mix. Daniel had been right; it looked like someone had raided Patrick's parents' spirits cabinet. We exchanged glances, like we both knew the soft drink option was not going to happen.

"I'll have the tropical stuff." I pointed to the bottle.

"Me too," Daniel said quickly, then flushed when Zoe and I smirked a bit, realising too late he had chosen the girliest drink on the counter. "Actually, I'll have a Jack and Coke."

"No problem." Zoe smiled sweetly. I wondered how she could appear so confident, yet quiet at the same time. It was a way of being I was keen to master. She wore her eyeliner in little cat flicks and had on a tight band t-shirt and black jeans, but somehow looked more dressy than me. Her nails were painted an electric blue, almost the same hue as her eyes.

From Daniel's frown I knew he had spotted Patrick or someone similar. I followed his line of sight and could see Patrick sitting beside Kara on a sofa in the conservatory, stroking her blonde curls. They looked lost in their own world.

I caught Zoe watching me. She averted her eyes, filling a frosted glass to the brim with pink tropical mix. As she poured a generous measure of bourbon into a half pint glass for Daniel I felt my palms begin to sweat. What if he got drunk and abandoned me?

"Cheers." Zoe handed us our glasses and picked up her own, downing the contents in one go.

I exchanged a nervous glance with Daniel, taking

a cautious sip.

"So, how are you liking Rowantree?" Zoe attempted conversation, pouring herself a fresh glass of tropical goodness.

"It's okay. A lot quieter than what I'm used to. But it's nice." I nodded, feeling like an idiot. I was very bad at small talk. "What about you, Zoe? How long have you lived here?"

"All my life." Zoe smiled ruefully. "I was born here, will no doubt die here."

Daniel's head shot up at that comment.

Zoe flushed. "I mean...my house has been in my family for generations, so if my little sister doesn't want it I'll probably move back here one day."

There was an awkward silence. I nudged Daniel and he scowled at me.

Say something, I mouthed.

His eyes screamed, *Like what?*

"Do you live with your parents?" I asked.

Zoe hesitated. "My dad. He works away a lot though, offshore."

"Cool," I nodded. "What does your mum do?"

A longer pause this time. "She died."

"Oh, sorry." My face flamed at my blunder. I silently cursed Daniel, thinking he could have warned me. He was too busy looking around the kitchen. I desperately tried to think of something else to say, to fill the awkward silence. I could see that I had upset Zoe and wondered if the death had been recent. "So, have Patrick and Kara lived here all their lives too?"

"Patrick has. Kara moved here when she was three. We all grew up together." Zoe paused. "Like one big happy family."

There was an edge to her voice at that comment. *Curious*. She also looked at Daniel when she said that, and I wondered how long he had lived here, if he had grown up with them too.

Daniel moved towards the fridge and I wondered what he was up to. He'd already devoured half the canapés at Mr Harris's exhibition; he surely couldn't still be hungry.

"This is a cool picture. D'you all go snowboarding a lot?" Daniel pointed at the photos pinned to the fridge door. I edged closer to see Kara, Patrick, Zoe and another girl and two boys I didn't recognise grinning into the camera, adorned in ski suits, boards and skis sticking out of a hill of snow behind them.

"Not so much since…you know…" Zoe's voice trailed off. "Louise's parents own a skiing lodge near the Alps and a cabin up North. All the families used to go weekend trips. They sometimes let us go to the cabin by ourselves now."

"Cool, are you a good skier?" Daniel turned to look at Zoe.

She shrugged. "I'm okay at snowboarding."

"She's being modest. Zoe is the best out of all of us – she should go pro." Patrick appeared in the doorway, chewing an unlit cigar, swirling ice round an empty glass. He slung an arm around Zoe's shoulder and her body visibly tensed. Patrick held up his glass, not taking his eyes off me as he said, "Fill me up, darling." A grin crept up his face as he took in my dress.

I gulped down half my drink. Daniel shot me a defiant look, taking an even bigger slug of his. I suppressed a laugh as his face contorted in disgust.

"Zoe, you should have brought Darcy and Daniel into the conservatory." Kara crept up behind me like a cat, touching me gently on the shoulder on her way past. She slunk towards Patrick, her silk top clinging to her hips as she walked. It dipped into a low V at the back, a smatter of glitter trailing down the dents of her spine, her skin sparkling under the lights. Mum would kill me if I left the house wearing a top like that.

"Happy birthday, Kara." I fumbled around my bag for the small gift I'd ordered online. I held up the package. "I got you a little thing."

"How sweet." She smiled. I couldn't tell if there was any sincerity behind it. She leaned back against Patrick, reaching up to steal his cigar. "Just leave it on the counter." Her tone was dismissive. I wished I hadn't bothered. Daniel mouthed, 'Suck-up.' I made a face at him.

There was an awkward moment when I realised all three of them – Patrick, Kara and Zoe – were watching me, almost studying me. Was I really that fascinating?

"Have you ever been snowboarding, Darcy?" Patrick asked.

I shook my head. "No. I used to skateboard a bit. But it's not really the same..."

"You should come along on one of our trips," he said.

Kara frowned up at him.

"Maybe. Thanks."

I took another gulp of my drink. I turned my attention back to the photos on the fridge. "Who are the others in your photo?" I asked, thinking they all looked like supermodels.

"My older siblings." As Patrick said this, I noticed the family similarities – striking blue eyes, golden hue to the hair, charming smiles.

"Our turn for questions." Patrick poured himself a fresh drink. My legs started to tremble and I wished I was sitting down.

"Do you have any brothers or sisters?" Patrick asked.

I shook my head.

"Do you have a boyfriend?"

I hesitated and saw Kara glance over at Daniel.

"No," I said, just as Kara shouted, "He's standing right there."

Daniel's face flamed. I could feel a blush creeping up my neck.

Kara giggled. "We've embarrassed them."

"We're just friends," I said.

Patrick grabbed the cigar from Kara and chewed on it. "What do you know about everything that happened here? Does it worry you, wondering what kind of village you've arrived in?"

Three sets of eyes were on me again – Kara, Zoe and Patrick. Daniel appeared to be fascinated by the remnants of drink in his glass.

"I followed some of Christian's trial." I shrugged, trying to appear casual about it all.

"Do you think he did it?" Patrick asked, his eyes challenging.

Daniel glowered at him.

"No, I don't." I stood up a bit straighter, looking Patrick in the eye. His gaze didn't waver.

"So, who did it then? *Was it Professor Plum in the bedroom with the dagger*?" He put on a posh English accent and Kara frowned at him.

"Don't be crass," she said.

Patrick drained his glass and turned his attention to Daniel. "Don't go believing everything emo tells you."

"I'm not an emo," Daniel practically spat.

Zoe put her hand on Patrick's. "Can we change

the subject now? This is supposed to be a party."

I picked up on her cue, wanting to escape any more interrogation.

"Can you show me where the bathroom is?" I directed the question at Zoe and she nodded, leading me out of the kitchen. I turned back to see Kara whispering to Patrick, as he squeezed her shoulder, drawing her back into the conservatory.

"Patrick can get a bit annoying when he's drunk," Zoe said.

"It's fine." I attempted a breezy smile.

"It's been a while since anyone new our age moved here. You're a novelty. We're all quite curious about you."

The idea that they even wanted to know anything about me, made me more nervous. There was no way I could match up to their cool snowboarding lifestyle. Maybe if I kept my mouth shut I could give off a 'new girl mystique' vibe.

We stopped at a half open door along the hallway, the distinct sound of someone throwing up coming from inside. Zoe wrinkled her nose. "Um, I think I'll take you to the bathroom upstairs."

"Yeah, thanks." I laughed nervously, following her up the winding staircase. Zoe took the stairs two at a time, her t-shirt hiking up at the back, revealing a black tattoo of a crow, although the beak seemed too large for a crow. It was creepy, whatever it was. I wondered if Zoe had lied about her age to get such an elaborate tattoo when she was only seventeen, like me. A few of them seemed to have tattoos, even Daniel.

But then there was an air of sophistication and something like privileged confidence surrounding a lot of the young people in the village. They were probably used to getting whatever they wanted.

As we turned another corner, the walls were lined with paintings and family photos. Patrick's parents looked as perfect as their children, like coiffed celebrities. "Patrick's parents must be pretty cool, letting him have a party here," I said.

"Oh, they don't know. They're away for the weekend in Paris. They sometimes go over there as it's near Louise's parents...the Marshalls, and Kara's parents. They all like to stay in touch."

"Right." I nodded. "What about his brothers and sister? Did they go too?"

"They're all away at Uni. His brothers are in Edinburgh and London, and his sister got some fashion internship in New York."

"Cool. That must be amazing."

"Yeah. Even cooler if your parents pay for your apartment. I think Patrick's going to move out to New York for a while after he finishes school."

Listening to Zoe made me realise even more how different their lives were to mine. It seemed weird having grown up about twenty minutes away from them. It may as well have been the other end of the world. I felt self-conscious about my unglamorous life.

Dad earned a good wage now after his promotion in London, but we had never been properly wealthy.

Zoe paused at an open door. The sound of a girl laughing loudly punctuated the air, music blaring from a stereo. "Roo?"

Zoe pushed the door wider, giving me a view into the chaos. Roo was dancing wildly, a spaghetti strap from her top sliding down her shoulder, hair shaking down her back as a boy nibbled hungrily on her neck, a half-empty bottle of Tequila leaking onto the carpet from his tilted hand.

Zoe grabbed Roo's arm, pulling her back from the boy.

The boy protested, his fingers holding tight around Roo's other wrist, giving her the appearance of a rag doll in a tug of war. Roo stumbled against her sister, a dreamy drunken smile on her face as she patted Zoe on the cheek. "Hey, sis. Always here to mop up my mess. Lucky me."

"You've had enough to drink, Roo. Come downstairs. I'll make you coffee."

"She's fine here, with me. Why don't you run along and ruin someone else's party?"

Zoe was fast, the force of her push taking me as much by surprise as the boy. He stumbled, sending the bottle smashing against a cabinet. "What the fuck?" Anger and humiliation burned in his eyes, but it was nothing compared to the rage on Zoe's face. "She's only fifteen. How old are you?"

The flash of shock and guilt was enough to reveal he was older. Probably much older.

"Call me," Roo slurred over her shoulder as Zoe dragged her out the room. Zoe barely looked at me on the way past, her tour guide mission forgotten.

I watched them retreat towards the staircase, a pang of sympathy knotting in my stomach as Roo's laughter exploded into tears, Zoe pulling her close, whispering in her ear, helping her walk. I thought back to what Zoe said in the kitchen and couldn't imagine losing mum at fifteen, or seventeen. Losing that anchor of safety.

I turned my back on them and noticed a room further along the hallway with a light on. I hesitated, taking in the boyish décor, shelves lined with books and trophies. I paused, then stepped inside, my eyes drawn to photo-booth pictures of Kara and Patrick pinned above the bed. I opened one of the desk drawers, not thinking about what I was doing, not really knowing what I was looking for.

The top drawer was full of pens, USBs, chewing gum, aftershave... I slammed it shut and opened the larger bottom drawer. A red box caught my attention – Louise was spelled out in sparkly stickers along the lid. I opened it to find it crammed full of photos – of Louise and Patrick, skiing trips, old photos where they looked about thirteen. More of Patrick with his siblings, a small brunette standing in the middle of them, smiling shyly. Zoe. Patrick had an arm around her, like he was a protective brother.

Then another one of Zoe, younger this time, dancing with a boy – a tall boy with dirty blonde hair and striking blue eyes. Christian...? I picked it up in surprise. He looked about twelve in the photograph. And then another one, which looked like Louise and Daniel grinning into the camera.

As I dug deeper into the box I found a couple of Polaroid photos of teenagers in Halloween costumes. One of Louise and Patrick – her face was painted white, her lips blood red. A chill ran up my back as I realised it had probably been taken the night she died. I picked up another – Zoe dressed as a zombie bride, a startled expression on her face, smudges of red down her cheeks. In the next, a gangster and a rabbit posed arm in arm.

But it was the boy in the shadows who caught my attention – he was wearing a ripped white sheet with red blotches down the front. I moved the photo under the light of the lamp; it looked like Christian.

A creak of floorboards out in the hall made my heart jump. I slid some of the photos into the pocket of my dress and quietly closed the drawer, just in time before the door swung open.

Chapter Ten

"Are you lost?"

Patrick loomed above me and I was conscious of the pulse in my throat throbbing in time with my heart. He edged closer, looking at my hands, as if he expected to catch me with something.

I desperately tried to think of an excuse as to why I was in his room. Then I noticed a large New York print on his wall. "I was just wondering if that photo was of Washington Square Park? I've always wanted to go to New York. Zoe said your sister is there and you might go out to stay for a while. Have you been before?" My words were all running into one and I knew he would never buy it.

He folded his arms. "No."

As he edged closer I lost my balance and stumbled onto his bed. Trying to act like my move was intentional, I crossed my legs awkwardly.

"You know, if you wanted me to take you to bed you only had to ask." He crouched beside me, the scent of whisky on his breath giving his words more of an edge.

I felt the heat from his body and noticed stubble running down the side of one cheek, like he still hadn't quite mastered the art of shaving. He gazed at my lips, his mouth parted slightly. I grabbed the edge of his duvet, wondering if he was actually going to attempt to kiss me.

His face cracked into a smile and he straightened up. "You look terrified, Darcy."

Flushing, I jumped up. "Yeah, well. It's scary having your face so close to mine."

As I brushed past him he grabbed my arm, his fingers tightening, nipping my skin.

"I'd rather you didn't snoop around my stuff," he said, his voice low and serious, all traces of flirtation gone. "It's not very polite."

I swallowed, waiting for him to loosen his grip.

"I get the feeling you're trying to poke your nose into a story that ended long ago. I think you should leave well alone."

He released me and I rubbed at my arm, the fear lessening and my anger sparking. "That sounds like a threat, Patrick."

"Let's just call it a friendly warning," he said. He looked pointedly at his door and I shuffled forward. Hurrying out to the hall, I collided with Daniel, who was exiting the bathroom. His eyes narrowed when he saw Patrick behind me.

"Alright, Danny boy." Patrick grinned as he swaggered down the stairs.

Daniel frowned. "Were you in his bedroom?"

I rolled my eyes. "I was snooping around and he sort of caught me."

Daniel tilted his head questioningly. "Did he try something?"

"No," I said quickly, the image of Patrick's face an inch from mine still fresh in my mind. "I don't think he was very happy with me." His change in character had been unsettling; one minute an arrogant flirt, the next almost aggressive. I thought back to what Zoe had said about him being annoying when he was drunk. Just annoying? Or did he sometimes get violent? Rumours had suggested this when he was under the spotlight in forums.

"So, did you actually find anything?" Daniel asked quietly as we headed downstairs.

"Nothing incriminating. Something I want to ask you about, though."

Kara and Zoe were hovering by the porch, watching us descend. Roo was lying down on a swing seat, bare feet pushing at the arm rest, cuddling a cushion to her chest. Zoe quickly pulled out her phone when we locked eyes. She turned her back to us, stroking Roo's hair and Kara returned to the kitchen.

"I think I want to go home, now," I whispered to Daniel.

"Fine by me. Let's go." Daniel strode towards the door and I grabbed his arm.

"We can't just leave without saying goodbye."

He made a face at me, then shouted to Zoe. "Hey, catch you later, Zoe."

She turned around in surprise. "Are you going already?"

"Yeah, night." He waved and was half way down the drive before I'd put on my jacket.

"Can you say thanks to Kara? See you at school on Monday." I smiled.

"Bye bye, Darcy. Don't do anything I would do," Roo waved and Zoe shushed her.

"See you." I sensed Zoe's gaze follow us all the way down the drive, out to the street.

My body breathed a sigh of relief when we turned the corner. "I don't think I enjoyed that much."

"Good."

I looked at Daniel curiously. "Why, good?"

"It means you won't drag me along to any more of those stupid nights."

"We might need to, though."

"No one needs to hang about with *them*."

"I still think if we get to know them a bit better

then they might start spilling some secrets." I thought back to the way Zoe opened up a bit as we'd climbed the stairs. She might tell me more if I could get her to trust me. "Zoe was quite friendly."

"Yeah, well, she's about the only half decent one."

"You could have warned me that she'd lost her mum. Was that recent?"

Daniel shrugged. "Yeah, a few months ago. I didn't think it would come up. She'd been ill for a long time. Christian mentioned something about it a few times - said something about him doing most of a project they were paired up for, because Zoe had to look after her mum. He was decent like that."

"Speaking of which…." I pulled out a couple of photos from my pocket, waving them teasingly in front of his face. "You and Louise look pretty friendly here. And Christian with Zoe."

"Let me see them." He grabbed at my hands, staring in wonder. "Where the hell did you find these? Look at my hair."

"Yeah, nearly as cool as now." I laughed.

"Hey." He tucked a strand behind his ear.

A goofy smile spread across his lips as he looked back at the photo. "I used to have a major crush on Louise in primary school."

"Really?"

"She liked me too." He handed the photo back to me. "But things changed when we all went to high school."

"Like how?" I asked, sliding the photo back into my pocket, thinking of the other one of Christian and Zoe.

"We just drifted apart. They all started getting drunk every weekend and went on their skiing trips.

Christian and me were more into music and watching films. We weren't cool enough for them."

I wondered if Christian had the same perception. It could be something to ask him about when I emailed again.

We reached the corner that led to Daniel's house and he hesitated.

"Do you want me to walk you home?" he asked.

"Nah, I'm just five minutes down the hill. See you Monday."

"Alright. Later, dude." He waved and I watched him jog out of sight.

*

When I turned the key to the flat I braced myself in case Mr Harris was inside with Mum. I was relieved to find the lights off, with no one home. I glanced at my watch. Eleven. The exhibition would be well over. They must have gone on somewhere. I wasn't sure if I was happy or weirded out – a bit of both, I decided.

I kicked off my shoes, massaging my squashed toes, and caught a glimpse of my reflection in the hall mirror on the walk to my room. My red curls had frizzed out a bit and my eye-liner had smudged below my eyes – actually giving me a bit of a cool grunge look.

As I padded around the flat the silence pressed down on me, a nagging reminder that things were different now. No Dad sitting watching TV in his chair. I glanced at our new IKEA furniture. He no longer had a chair in our house. I tried to bury the thought, grabbing snacks from the kitchen and heading to my bedroom, clicking on music. Too much quiet sent my mind racing.

Snuggling into bed I fired up my netbook, logging

into the prisoner email site. I spread Christian's letter open beside me, along with the photo of him and Zoe. I scrutinised it, figuring they must be about eleven or twelve.

Dear Christian,

Thanks for writing back. I know it must be weird receiving emails from someone you don't know– I guess I didn't really think about the strange mail you might receive. You were quite blunt in your letter about the 'convicted murderer' statement – it surprised me. I thought you would never want to call yourself that. Have you given up trying to prove you're innocent? Or was it a test? I don't scare easily, just so you know.

I paused, thinking of Patrick's warning.

So, I'm just back from a party at Patrick Barrington's house. I know he's probably not your favourite person. Daniel came with me, but don't worry – he didn't actually want to go. I made him. Kara hasn't exactly been putting out a welcoming committee for me, so I thought it might make things a bit easier if I got to know them all a bit better. Also, I guess I should tell you that I'm thinking maybe I can find some answers... I didn't say in my first email, but I have big doubts about your whole case. I think the way you were treated was pretty bad. We followed a bit of your trial at my old school, looking at the forums and podcasts. I continued to follow parts of it. I'm still reading up on it just now, and there seems to be a lot of unanswered questions. If *I* feel like that, then you must be going mad, wanting answers?

I found a photo of you and Zoe at Patrick's. You look about eleven or twelve? You're both wearing hats and you're smiling. I also found a photo of Daniel and Louise. Daniel mentioned that they liked each other in primary school but things started to change when you all went to high school. Were you all close friends at one point? What do you think changed?

I also went along to an exhibition this evening – it was your art teacher's, Mr Harris. He's pretty cool. Your mum turned up actually. So I got to meet her. Does she visit you much? She seemed a bit sad. I guess it must be really hard for her. Do you have any brothers or sisters? I'm guessing you don't, as I don't remember reading about them. I don't have any siblings. I kind of wish I did a lot of the time. Though I guess if I had a sister it could be annoying – you know, if she tried to borrow my clothes and stuff.

Anyway, I'd better sign off now.

Darcy

I read over it twice, then hit send before I over-analysed every word. I checked the time. Midnight. Where was Mum? On cue, my phone rang, making me jump.

"Young lady, I hope you are home and in bed," Mum said.

"I am. Like a total loser."

"How was the party?"

"Fine," I said. "Where are you?"

"Just about to drive home. Timothy – Mr Harris – took me to see a very intellectual documentary."

"Did it have subtitles?" I grinned. Mum hated films with subtitles.

"No. All in plain American English."

"Great, you can tell me all about it in the morning."

"Alright, sweetie. I'll be home soon."

"Night." I clicked off, suddenly having the urge to phone Dad. I stared at my phone for a good ten minutes, re-reading some of his messages. A loneliness gnawed at me as I pictured Dad living his new life in London, without me. He was probably out on a date too, with his assistant. Both of my parents were having fun and here I was, alone in the dark in a place that didn't feel like home yet. I grabbed at my quilt, making a fist. It didn't seem fair. Then I thought of Christian, locked in his cell. No matter how alone and miserable I felt, it must be nothing compared to what he was dealing with. The thought calmed me, and I picked up my phone again, taking a deep breath.

Then, before I changed my mind, I quickly typed:

Hi Dad. School is going ok.

I started to type:

I miss you

…but deleted those three words, tears stinging my eyes. It was so much easier staying angry at him; it lessened the stabbing pain of his absence. I hit *Send* then switched off my phone, curling into a ball and crying myself to sleep.

Post-Murder: Scene One

A buzzing noise invaded Christian's dream. As he opened his eyes, the anxiety and fear he had felt in his nightmare didn't properly subside. He felt around for his phone and realised blood had dripped from the scratches on his arm onto his bed sheets during the night. He gulped back a wave of nausea.

"Hello?" He spoke into the phone, closing his eyes again.

"Christian? Did you hear, man? Can you believe it?"

"Believe what?" He sighed, moving back under the covers, wondering what time it was.

"It's Louise. She was found out on her parents' balcony in the early hours...someone stabbed her..."

A chill shot through Christian's body.

Daniel's words ran together too fast, parts jumping out. *"...there's police and some kind of forensic investigators all over the street...and cameras, the journalists are already knocking doors. It's insane, man."*

Christian felt sick. An image of Louise flashed in his head, her white dress fanning out as he spun her round, under his arm, around and around...

"Christian?"

He blinked, realising Daniel was waiting for him to answer a question he hadn't heard. "Yeah?"

"Where did you disappear to last night? I was looking for you and you never answered my messages."

"Oh, yeah. Sorry." Christian held his arm up, his eyes following the scratches down to his wrist.

Silence. He realised Daniel was waiting for him to explain more.

"I…ran into Patrick and he was being an arse, like always. I left early."

"I figured." Daniel said. *"What you up to today? Want to come over? I can't believe this happened."*

Christian hesitated. "Have they taken her to hospital?"

A pause. *"No, man. She's, um, dead."*

"Oh. Shit."

The phone started to shake in Christian's hand. "For real?"

"For real."

"I'll come over later."

"Okay. Later."

Christian lay back down on his bed, staring at his phone. He hesitated, then scrolled down through his contacts, stopping at a name he really wanted to talk to. His finger hovered over the green call symbol, then he changed his mind, the call failing to connect.

He sat up, switching on the lamp, fumbling around in the bedside cabinet drawer for cigarettes. He pulled one out the pack, placing it between his trembling lips. How could someone be so alive one minute, then dead, just like that? When he blinked he could see Louise's smiling face, her laughter still in his ears.

Christian picked up his lighter, the flame creating a welcome glow. As a soothing surge of nicotine flowed through him, he spun the lighter in his hand and looked down to see the initials CH, stained red. Blood red.

You shouldn't have gone back. The words raged in his head as he dropped the lighter into a glass of water, washing the stains away.

Chapter Eleven

Dear Teen sleuth,

Congratulations on making it out of a Patrick Barrington party alive. I need to maintain a sense of humour about him. I'm trying to picture this photo of me and Zoe that you mention. And the one of Louise with Daniel – Daniel's hair was always a riot (still is). A part of me wants you to post them to me, but these things get intercepted and can you imagine how that could mess with my appeal, if the guards were to find a photo of Louise in here? The police and their prosecutor created a nice little story about my obsession with her, and how it fuelled my anger when she 'rejected' me that night. But I guess if you followed my trial as closely as you say you did, you'll already know all of that.

Of course I get angry. But the longer I'm here, the more I realise that I've got to let go of that anger, to reach some level of acceptance. Or I will just go insane. I'm not sure what you hope to achieve? *Are* you some super teen sleuth? You do know I had a pretty smart solicitor and advocate working my case, and Mum has also linked in with some Justice Party people. They've not really achieved much, apart from building some more awareness of my case, attempting to paint a better picture of who I am. No one wants to come forward with any truths from that night – truth is sometimes complicated though, don't you think? So back to that photo...When I first moved to Rowantree I was different — more open and likeable I guess. Louise and Zoe and Kara were also different — sweet and uncomplicated. Weirdly enough, me and Louise were almost best friends at one point. I changed when my dad left me and Mum. I was only eleven and I was really angry — it felt like he'd abandoned us. I've only just started to process that time in my head now.

I have a lot of hours in here to think over too many things. I guess I never realised how much it did affect me.

I think I started to ignore Louise before she ignored me. I reckon that pissed her off a bit, as she hated to be ignored. She became super aware of how pretty she was and was really manipulative with it. And that became really annoying. She always seemed to want to rule over everyone, especially her cousin, Kara. It was like she always needed to prove to everyone she was the prettiest, the coolest.

By the time we were fourteen — a year before she died — we were like strangers. And Kara, Patrick and his siblings — they all turned into shallow idiots. Their families are all way too close — most of their parents grew up together and are pretty dysfunctional.

To answer your other question — I do have a sister — a step-sister. She was born a year and a half ago. It's partly why my Dad never showed up to see any of my trial. A convenient excuse I think. I hope I get to meet her one day.

Later,

Christian Henderson

I sat re-reading the last paragraph, my hands turning ice cold, the words step-sister popping off the page. I realised I had been suppressing fears of something similar happening to me. What if Dad stayed with his personal assistant? What if he started a new family without me? I couldn't imagine how that must have felt for Christian, going through a horrific trial, knowing his dad wasn't there to support him, knowing he was too busy loving someone else.

I'd received a long email from Dad after I'd messaged him, telling me lots about his work and a camping expedition he went on, taking care not to mention anything about his new girlfriend, though I suspected she accompanied him on the trip. He asked if I wanted to go down to stay with him during the October break, suggesting he could take me to see a musical of my choice. But there was no way I was ready.

I scanned back over Christian's letter, trying to form a clearer picture of Louise – manipulative and controlling. From photos I'd seen she looked very similar to Kara but did seem to have an edge, a more brazen smile. Maybe she pushed people too far...

A knock on my door caused me to half jump out my skin.

"I'm off out to dinner," Mum called, popping her head round just as I slid the letter under my leg. "What you up to?"

"Homework," I lied. I had only just managed to grab the post before Mum that morning. Christian had replied more quickly this time, which surprised me as Daniel said he hadn't heard from him again. I leaned forward, getting a proper look at Mum's tight jeans and top. "Are you off out with my teacher?"

Mum hesitated. "Maybe."

"Have fun," I said. "Tell him to give me an A for the rest of the year," I shouted after her. Once she was gone I read Christian's letter once more then hid it in my jewellery box, already constructing a response in my head.

*

The next morning, I was surprised to find Kara waiting for me downstairs. The smile on her lips made me uneasy. We walked in near silence to the bus stop until she piped up:

"Did your mum enjoy her date last night?"

I looked at her in shock. How did she know? "Um, she wasn't on a date."

Kara raised a perfectly groomed eyebrow. "Oh, really. It's just I saw Mr Harris kissing her in his car when he dropped her home last night. Must just be good pals then, eh?"

A mixture of rage and embarrassment shot through me. How could Mum be so stupid? If she was going to kiss my teacher in public, didn't she know not to do it right on our doorstop in front of flipping Kara Stephenson?

I didn't know what to say in response so instead I walked away, relieved to find Daniel sitting on the bench at the bus stop. His eyes were questioning when he saw the expression on my face.

"Everything okay?"

I let out a long sigh. "Just Mum being stupid. Kara saw her and Mr Harris kissing."

"Oh." Daniel looked surprised. "They're still seeing each other then?"

I nodded glumly. Kara pressed up against Patrick, smirking at me. At least she wasn't in my Art class. A small mercy. Suddenly the thought of Mum with Mr Harris seemed all a bit too real. I pulled my jacket tighter around me. *Why did everything have to keep changing?*

As we stepped onto the bus, Zoe arrived just as the doors were shutting. She banged on them loudly to stop the driver setting off without her. As she walked past us I noted her pale face. She looked like she hadn't slept, her make-up doing little to disguise the shadows under her eyes. "Rough night?" I heard Patrick ask, but it wasn't in a jokey way, like his usual self.

I heard Zoe mumble something, catching the words, 'Dad not helping. She was brought home in a police car. She can't keep doing this...' Kara slid into the seat next to her, obscuring my view. I thought I could hear sobs, so I turned away, not wanting to invade her privacy. I realised Roo wasn't with her this morning and guessed she had been talking about her, wondering what trouble she'd got into.

For such a small village we were all pretty messed up. Daniel nodded his head in time with the tunes blasting in his ears, completely oblivious to Zoe's anguish, staring off into nothing as the bus trundled out the village. He seemed the most balanced of us all. I could see why Christian liked being his friend. He emanated a sense of calm, which was reassuring amongst the chaos.

I pulled out my phone and started to compose an angry message to Mum, then thought better of it and deleted my words.

As we walked through the school doors I realised I had Art second period. I was angry at Mr Harris too – he was the last person I wanted to see. In English, Zoe and Kara were missing. No one seemed to care or notice. A restlessness stirred inside me, the word 'escape' circling my head. When the bell rang I slipped away from Daniel, telling him I was going to the toilet.

Instead, I headed outside, hurrying down the path to the main gates. As I turned a corner onto the street I nearly walked straight into Zoe and Kara, who were sharing a bag of crisps.

"Little Miss Perfect playing truant too?" Kara smiled wryly.

I frowned. "You don't know anything about me."

"Oh yeah?" Kara folded her arms, a smirk playing on her lips. A flush snaked up my neck at her scrutiny.

She hesitated then held out the bag of crisps. "Want to join us then? We're heading into the city for some girl time."

I blinked in surprise, then took a crisp, feeling a surge of excitement at the prospect of ditching school and going off on an adventure. But with them? Did they really want me to tag along? My phone beeped and I glanced at the message.

Have your bowels exploded or what? Mr Harris is asking where you are.

I switched off my phone thinking Mr Harris could feck off. Escaping for the day with Zoe and Kara seemed like my best option.

"Come on, the next train leaves in five minutes." Zoe grabbed my arm and pulled me along the road behind them, the click of their heels echoing all the way down the street in time with their breathless laughter. Their exuberance was contagious. I found myself running alongside them.

In town, I relaxed in the comforting sense of

familiarity – the hiss of buses, the bustle of crowds, horns beeping. I realised I had missed the noise and vibrancy of it all. After trying on hideous dresses in a designer shop, Kara pulled us into a burger bar.

"So, spill, then. Tell us what brought you to Rowantree," Kara said.

They sat watching me intently as I told my story, Zoe chewing on the ice from her milkshake. Their matching green eyeshadow glittered under the harsh lights every time they blinked. I was self-conscious at first; I hadn't even told Fee the whole story with mum and dad. The fact Kara and Zoe didn't really know me, or my family, made it easier.

"Parents are right dicks sometimes," Kara murmured. "My mum's deepest relationship is with the bottom of a vodka bottle. My dad is so concerned with trying to save her he tends to forget I even exist. I'm glad they moved to France. My gran is okay though, she's pretty sound."

I waited for Zoe to say something about her dad and sister, but she turned her attention back to me instead. "I can't believe that your mum would date your bloody art teacher. It's kind of crass."

An emotion like guilt stirred inside me, but then I thought about Mum kissing Mr Harris in full view of Kara and I brushed it aside. "Tell me about it. And my dad's new girlfriend is half his age. He's such a loser."

I noticed Kara scrutinising me, like she was trying to weigh something up. I took a nervous sip of my Coke, distracting myself from her unnerving gaze.

"You know, Mr Harris is a bit of a letch," Kara said.

I looked up in surprise. "What do you mean?"

"A while back, when Louise was in third year, he

got a bit handsy with her."

A sick feeling hit the pit of my stomach. "He what?"

"Kara," Zoe snapped. "That was a load of BS and you know it."

Kara arched her eyebrow, shrugging nonchalantly. "He was questioned about it. And Louise cried about it too."

Zoe shook her head, her expression darkening. "Louise was a manipulative schemer. She wanted attention – you always said that too. She loved spinning lies, creating drama."

They locked eyes and Kara held up her hands. "You're right, she was manipulative. I shouldn't have mentioned it."

We all sat in despondent silence, our half-eaten burgers sitting in a sodden mess on our plates.

Kara reached into her purse and pulled out a crisp twenty, her eyes lighting up as she grinned. "Here's one good thing about having dysfunctional parents. They send me guilt money every couple of weeks from their French château. Let's hit the offie on the way home and drink wine under the stars."

"Yes!" Zoe jumped up. "You've got to see the view from the hills behind our houses, Darcy. It's beautiful. We'll be able to see Venus tonight."

Kara rolled her eyes. "Alright, Annie Astronomy." She laughed as we headed up the street, ripping off her school tie and zipping up her leather jacket. She pulled out a compact and pouted as she filled in her lips with red gloss. We followed her to the off licence, obeying as she ordered us to wait outside, knowing that we had no hope of fooling the guy behind the counter.

"She's never going to pass for twenty-five," I

murmured to Zoe, watching as Kara strode up and down the aisles, her hips swaying deliberately as she walked.

Zoe grinned. "Just watch. She knows how to play them."

I watched in interest – the cashier was no longer reading his magazine, instead unsubtly checking out Kara as she strained to reach a bottle of red wine on the top shelf. He hurried out from behind the counter, going to her aid.

Zoe chuckled. "Sucked in. She's done it."

Ten minutes later Kara emerged with three bottles of wine and his phone number.

"Loser." She laughed, ripping up the paper, the wind catching the shreds, which trailed after us like confetti as we ran back towards the station.

As Zoe linked her arm through mine I felt a wave of invincibility – strangers' gazes strayed towards us as we powered through the crowds, as if a magnetic energy radiated from us.

My phone vibrated in my pocket, pulling me back to reality. I slid it out, seeing 'Mum' flash up on the screen and a few more messages from Daniel along the lines of:

Where are you??

I quickly typed a response to Daniel:

Felt sick – went home early. Talk later.

I switched it off without responding to Mum's call.

By the time we got back to Rowantree it was early

evening and dark enough to see the stars. Zoe led the way to the top of Lomond Drive, past rows of houses with matching sports cars at the tops of winding drives. We huddled close, the chill of the wind burning my cheeks.

I pulled my scarf up to my nose as we climbed over a wooden fence at the end of a cul-de-sac, leading us up to the hills behind the village. Kara handed the bottles of wine to Zoe as she launched herself over the fence.

Zoe started to unscrew the lid of one bottle as she led us further up into the darkness, the moon lighting a faded path for us. A shiver of excitement filled me as I looked down at the houses and lights dotted beneath us, the village becoming a miniature version of itself. As Zoe climbed to the peak of a grassy verge, she held up the bottle in a cheers gesture, before taking a swig and passing it on to me.

I hesitated, then let the vinegary liquid slide down my throat. It felt good forgetting everything for a while, silencing the anger at mum, burying thoughts of dad's absence even deeper inside.

Kara plonked herself down beside me.

"Sorry about earlier, with the thing I said about Mr Harris."

I shook my head in surprise, indicating it was no big deal.

"Zoe was right when she said Louise could be a manipulative schemer sometimes. She liked to stir things and didn't care about the consequences." Kara gestured to Zoe, who was squinting up at the sky, whilst unscrewing another bottle of wine. "Zoe knows that better than anyone."

"What do you mean?" I asked.

Kara grabbed the bottle from me, red wine

staining her chin as she drank too fast. She wiped at the drips and shook her head. "Louise was twisted. She claimed that Zoe's dad flirted with her at one of our family's gatherings – that he enjoyed talking to her and got so lonely with his wife being ill." Kara's expression darkened. "We already knew Zoe was struggling – that her dad did nothing to help and left money for Zoe to take her mum to hospital in taxis. And Roo is always playing up, and her dad leaves Zoe to deal with that too. It was the last thing Zoe needed to hear. I don't know what Louise was playing at."

I watched Zoe, feeling a pang of sympathy for her. Louise did sound spiteful.

"Were you close to Louise?" I asked.

Kara shrugged. "I guess she was like a sister to me. Neither sets of our parents are…were…very present in our lives." Kara's usual aloofness softened, making her appear younger. "She could be horrible to me too though. She got so jealous sometimes, if I got too much attention from boys." Kara looked up as Zoe approached. "She was really weird with Zoe too after she caught her kissing…"

"Kara," Zoe interrupted, swooping down to grab the bottle of wine from Kara's hand, clinking it against her own. "Let's not bore Darcy with stories of a time when we were young and stupid."

Kara watched Zoe down the wine, a trace of sadness in her smile.

I followed her gaze. "Is Zoe like a sister to you too?"

Kara hesitated. "I guess so. We all look out for one another, you know?" I detected a flicker of a challenge in her eyes. Was that a warning? That they would all stick together, no matter what?

Kara jumped up and grabbed Zoe's hand, pulling her up the hill. I tilted my head back to look up at the sky, which kept exploding with more and more stars the longer I looked. Maybe when you're faced with total darkness, it's only then you can start to see the light. I looked over at Zoe and Kara and wanted to speak those words out loud, thinking I had discovered some profound answer hidden in the sky. They were laughing hysterically at some impression Kara was doing of a teacher and I decided I should save those words for Christian.

But where was his light? Could I really help him find it?

Chapter Twelve

Dear Christian,

Thanks for your letter. I'm writing this to you on top of a hilltop in the freezing cold, with Rowantree below me. My fingers are going a bit numb and I'm using the torch on my phone as a light as I scribble this in my notebook, so excuse the handwriting. I can see lots of little miniature mansions, with lights shining in the windows, illuminating toy cars and tall fences which I think are designed to keep out burglars, but really they look like they're locking people in, isolating them from the world.

I'm here with Zoe and Kara. (I know, I know). We're drinking wine (it tastes awful). They're actually OK. I told them a bit about my dad. It felt good talking to someone. I know what you mean when you say you feel like your dad abandoned you. I feel like that about my dad. I don't think I could handle it if he had a baby with his new girlfriend. I'm sorry your dad wasn't there for you during your trial. That must have been really hard. I think it's nice you say you want to meet your step-sister. I hope you do get to meet her one day.

It must have been really hard for your mum when you were brought to trial. And it must have been terrifying for you both the day you were arrested. Your mum seemed very protective of you the day I met her. It made me think how my mum would have reacted in that situation - I think she would have probably tried to punch one of the police officers. It's pretty amazing up here. I can't remember the last time I saw the stars so clearly. And the air seems so fresh here. I'm sorry. I bet that's something you miss. Do you get to go outside at all? I was going to write some cheesy line about darkness and light, but I think I'll save that one for another time.

I don't know what I think I can achieve. I always like to dig for the truth, to solve puzzles. There seems to be so many parts of your puzzle that were never really solved.

I'm beginning to understand when you say the families here are a bit dysfunctional. Kara told me a bit about her parents. And I found out that Zoe lost her mum – that must have been hard, though she hasn't really told me much about it. I've not met Daniel's parents yet, but I have a hunch they might be OK. What about Patrick's parents? What are they like?

I skipped school this afternoon. Mainly to avoid Mr Harris. Here's another thing we have in common – he's dating my mum. Weird, eh. How was that for you?

My head is starting to spin a bit. I'd better go. Mum is going to be so mad with me.

Later,

Darcy x

*

Mum opened the door before I'd even turned the key. Her eyes burned with the deadly fire that had the ability to make my knees quake without her saying a word.

114

"Sit down." She gestured towards the sofa and shut the door.

The room began to spin as I walked across the carpet. I could feel the burger from earlier sloshing around in my gut with the wine. I gagged.

Mum hesitated. "Are you ill?"

I shook my head, squeezing my eyes shut.

I could sense her behind me.

"Darcy, have you been drinking?"

A smaller shake of my head.

She sighed loudly. "I can smell it."

"I don't want to talk to you right now," I said.

"Oh, you don't want to talk to me? That much is obvious when you ignored my five phone calls and ten messages. When Timothy told me you hadn't turned up to class then you didn't appear home, didn't you think I'd be worried…?"

"I don't care what TIMOTHY thinks!" I shouted. "I don't want to talk to you right now."

Mum recoiled, taken aback by my outburst. A flicker of panic flashed across her face, before the anger returned.

"Don't you shout at me! Don't you know how worried I've been, wondering where you disappeared to? This isn't you, Darcy. We have an agreement, remember…honesty, respect?"

I guffawed. "Respect? You broke that agreement when you kissed my friggin' teacher right in front of one of my friends."

A look of shock and realisation dawned on Mum's face. Then the guilt. "Oh…last night? I'm sorry, I didn't think."

"Yes, last night," I said. "I don't want to talk about this just now. I want to go to bed. Please, just let me go to bed."

I was relieved when she didn't try to stop me or follow me down the hall. I slammed my door shut and threw myself face down on the bed, my head spinning faster and faster, in time with the anger-fuelled adrenaline pumping through my veins.

A wave of nausea overwhelmed me as I turned over on my side.

Don't throw up, don't throw up, I commanded my body, sliding the bin over beside me, just in case. Pulling the quilt up over my head, I drifted off into a strange half sleep, images of stars, and Zoe and Kara laughing, spinning through fractured dreams.

*

I woke to the smell of coffee and an assault of sunshine streaming in through the open curtains.

"Morning!" Mum trilled, thrusting a steaming mug of coffee under my nose. "Welcome to part one of your punishment."

I grimaced, trying to hide my face beneath my pillow.

"Uh, uh." Mum pulled the pillow right off my bed. "Up straight, get this down you and into the shower in five. I'm taking you to school this morning."

A rage of pain thundered in my head. "I'm too ill to go to school," I mumbled, pushing her hand away. "And you know I hate coffee."

"Drink," Mum ordered. "You'll thank me somewhere around ten this morning."

I took a sip, glaring at her. "I'm still not talking to you."

"Fine. We can fight about that one later." Mum shrugged. "For what it's worth, I apologise for being indiscreet – that was thoughtless of us. But I'm really not impressed with this acting out, Darcy. You should wait until you're at least forty before you use alcohol as a way of dealing with unpleasant emotions." She threw my bath towel onto the foot of the bed. I looked down to see I'd slept in my school skirt and shirt. I felt sweaty and disgusting and ill.

*

We drove to school in silence. I stared out the window the whole way, thankful I at least didn't have Art today.

"Straight home, then we can talk," Mum said as we pulled into the car park.

I nodded and clambered out of Wanda, relieved to breathe in some fresh air. I took my time walking, hoping the nausea would die down by the time I got to first period. My hand kept moving towards the front pocket of my bag, where I had tucked away Christian's letter to post later. It would probably surprise him, getting a handwritten letter this time. I liked it. It seemed more personal.

"Duuuude." Daniel appeared in my face. "I thought you weren't coming in when you weren't on the bus."

I recoiled, his voice too loud for me to deal with. "I'm delicate. Be gentle please."

"You do look a bit rough, mate. Still ill then?"

I didn't answer, walking on ahead.

"Everything okay?" he asked.

"Yeah, everything is brilliant," I said.

"Right-o. See you in English second period!" he called, hurrying off to his first class.

"Hey, Darcy." Zoe sat down next to me. "We thought you weren't coming in today."

"Oh, hi." I looked at her in surprise, wondering how she could possibly be so fresh faced and chirpy. "Are you immune to hangovers or something?"

Zoe smiled brightly. "I drank a whole load of water when I got home. Kara stayed at mine. I always sleep better when someone else is around, so that helped too."

I remembered Zoe said her dad worked away a lot. I wondered if she and her sister were left alone during those times. That must be awful, when they had lost their mum too. It made me feel stupid for making such a big deal of Mum's kiss. At least she was there for me. Things could be a lot worse.

The morning crawled by. At lunch, Daniel was waiting for me as usual in the canteen. There was an awkward moment when I realised that Zoe and Kara were motioning for me to sit with them and Patrick. Daniel raised an eyebrow. "Since when did they want to be your lunch buddies?"

I shrugged. "Maybe we should join them?"

His expression screamed, *Do I have to?*

"Come on, let's pretend to be at least a bit sociable."

"Fine." Daniel shrugged, following me to their table.

"How's your hangover, Darcy?" Patrick smirked as I sat down across from him.

I ignored him and also avoided Daniel's questioning stare.

Kara and Zoe were discussing a trip to the cabin up North for the October holiday.

"Are your brothers home then, Patrick?" Zoe asked.

Patrick shook his head. "They're going to see Ally in New York, I think. Is Roo coming with us this time?"

"Nah, her best friend has invited her to go away with her family, so it'll just be us lot again.

118

Apparently she was 'bored out her mind' the weekend we visited recently, because it rained so much and you know she hates me telling her what to do."

Zoe paused and smiled across the table at me. "You should come along on this trip, Darcy." Daniel tensed beside me.

"You too, Daniel." Zoe quickly added.

"I'll see. There's a chance I might have to go to see my Dad in London," I said.

Neither option was particularly appealing. The idea of being stuck in a remote cabin with Patrick and Kara for a week was a bit unnerving. I also couldn't imagine Mum being thrilled with me going away with a bunch of teenagers she didn't know without parental supervision.

Patrick leaned across the table. "Don't look so worried, Darcy. There's rarely any snow in October, so you'll be able to avoid the slopes."

I smiled in response, conscious of the fact that Daniel was sitting in silence. Even with my attempts to include him, he barely looked up from his chips. When the bell rang, he couldn't get out the canteen fast enough. I tried to walk by his side, but he kept hurrying ahead.

"Hey." I grabbed at his backpack, forcing him to slow down. "What's up with you?"

Daniel sighed loudly. "Look, I don't care if you'd rather hang around with them, but don't force me to, okay?"

I thought about trying to convince him that the girls weren't so bad, but the stubborn look on his face told me it wasn't going to make the slightest bit of difference.

"Alright, I won't. What you up to tonight?"

He shrugged. "Stuff. Homework."

"Want to come over to mine? I think I'll be grounded for a while."

"Why's that?" Daniel frowned, and I realised that I didn't want to share the story of my outing.

I shrugged. "Just an argument with Mum. Say you'll come over?"

"Okay," he agreed.

As we turned the corner, we nearly collided with Mr Harris.

"Darcy." Mr Harris nodded his head in acknowledgement, his expression hard to read. "Glad to see you're feeling better today."

I was relieved he didn't wait for a response and walked on. My hand traced along the material of my bag as I thought back to my letter to Christian. How had he felt when his mum had dated Mr Harris? It was a bit weird that Mr Harris was yet again dating one of his students' mums. Although Kara had backtracked a bit with the 'handsy' comments, they still bothered me. I watched Mr Harris walk the rest of the way down the corridor. Nothing about his demeanour was in the least bit creepy, but he could be good at fooling people. Maybe Christian would give me some answers in his next reply.

As I approached the next class, I felt my phone beep in my pocket. I pulled it out, seeing a message pop up.

PRIVATE MESSAGE to Darcy Thomas
From: Edgar
You think you're smart, but you're not as smart as me. Stop looking for answers. I'm watching you.

Chapter Thirteen

Mum brought home take-away and my anger towards her melted as she slid a can of cold Irn-Bru towards me along the kitchen counter.

"For making it through a day of school with a hangover. Your last EVER hangover while you're at school, I'd like to add." She looked at me sternly and I smiled, nodding in agreement.

"Should I stop seeing Mr Harris for a while?" she asked, dividing the chow mein onto plates, not making eye contact.

I paused mid sip, Irn-Bru fizz shooting up my nose. I was surprised Mum would consider that an option. Even though Kara and Zoe had basically dismissed Louise's story, what if there was some truth in it? A selfish part of me wanted to say yes, to keep Mum to myself, to stop the changes around us happening so fast. But if Dad got to be happy, surely it was only fair she did too.

"Are you enjoying spending time with him?" I asked.

"Very much so," she nodded. "He's an interesting man."

"A nice guy? Like, trustworthy?"

Mum hesitated, "Yes, I'd say so. Don't you think?"

I shrugged. "I don't think either of us know him that well yet. I just want you to be careful."

Mum ruffled my hair. "That's sweet, Darcy. But you're right – we don't know him that well, so I'm not going to be speeding ahead with anything, okay?"

I nodded. "Okay. I don't mind you still seeing

him, just not so many public displays of affection…"

"Noted." Mum handed me my plate. "And you promise no more skipping school and drinking with those girls?"

"Promise." I nodded, following her through to the living room. I checked my phone again, expecting another message to pop up. I was desperate for clues as to who Edgar might be, but also on edge. What if they became more threatening? I put my phone on silent, pleased to have a distraction now Mum was home.

We sat watching cheesy reality fashion shows, laughing at the ludicrous contestants. When the buzzer went, Mum frowned and I jumped up. "I totally forgot I invited Daniel round."

"Oh, did you?" Mum raised an eyebrow.

"Sorry." I stammered. "I thought I'd be grounded, and he was feeling a bit miserable at lunch today and I…"

"It's fine, Darcy. He can have some leftovers." Mum disappeared into the kitchen as I opened the door. Daniel seemed even taller as he entered our small abode. He also looked ridiculously awkward, hands stuffed in his pockets, a blush spreading across his face when Mum appeared grinning from ear to ear, handing him a plate of food.

"Take a seat, Daniel." She motioned to the sofa and set the plate down in front of him. "Have you eaten?"

"Um, yeah." He looked approvingly at the Chinese. "But this looks way better than the chicken and avocado salad Mum made."

"Ava-what-o?" Mum screwed up her nose and I rolled my eyes.

Daniel's awkwardness disappeared as he tucked

into the food. We watched some more of the crazy fashion show and Mum filled Daniel in on all of the contestants' finer qualities.

He turned to me at one point. "Your house is much more fun than mine."

It gave me a little glow when he said that, like it was a reassurance. I had been worried that without Dad there would be a massive dark hole eroding all sense of home. I still hadn't got used to not having him around, hassling me about homework and making sure I ate properly, but glancing at Mum, her cheeks flushed from laugher, feet tucked under her legs, I realised that her vibrancy had returned, and the flat felt warm because of it. Things had been so tense in our old house that we had all tended to avoid each other and there had been no joking around, no animated conversation over dinner like the old days. It was the old days I pined for really. It was a relief to see Mum back to normal. I hadn't realised how unhappy she'd been.

"Let's watch that celebrity confession show," Mum said, reaching for the remote.

"Uh, we have homework to do, Mum." I tugged at Daniel's sleeve. "I think Daniel's been subjected to enough trash for one night." I led him along the corridor to my room and shut the door on Mum's mad cackles. Daniel stood looking around, his eyes trailing across my bookcase, then to the heap of clothes on my bed. I dived forward, hiding a bra under a t-shirt, carrying the pile over to my washing basket.

"You've dropped something." I was aware of Daniel stretching forward and I prayed it wasn't for a pair of my knickers.

I was relieved to see he was holding what looked like photographs. I frowned, wondering where they were from, then realised I was holding the dress I'd worn to Patrick's party, the pockets gaping open.

"Where did you get these?" Daniel sat down, scrutinising the images. "It's Zoe... It looks like Louise's party." His face paled as he flicked to the one of Christian, a flash of confusion and almost worry in his expression. He looked at me, waiting for an answer.

"I forgot I'd put them in my pocket. I found them in that box...at Patrick's party, along with those other photos I showed you – the ones when you were about twelve."

Daniel stared again at the photo, like he wasn't quite believing what he was seeing. "I don't understand. I'm sure that's Christian in this one...but he's wearing a different outfit."

"What do you mean?" I dumped the clothes and sat down beside Daniel, pulling the photo towards me, scrutinising it. "It's like he's wrapped in a sheet. Maybe he's just larking about."

Daniel shook his head. "He was wearing a pirate outfit. He had on a wig and head scarf and everything. He's not wearing any of that here."

I waited for Daniel to say more; he seemed to have a million thoughts running through his head.

"I remember..." His voice trailed off.

"You remember what?" I prompted.

He sighed. "It was on one of those forums, where people were speculating about that night at the party. One guy kept insisting that Christian had been dressed as a ghost, walking around in a white sheet, with blood-red make-up streaked over it. People dismissed him, me included, insisting that he was a pirate. I've got extracts of forum posts in a folder on my laptop. I want to check back over them..." Daniel stood.

"Are you leaving?" I jumped up. "Can I come with you?"

"Didn't you say you were grounded?"

I shrugged. "Your house is only five minutes away. We can say that you left some important homework research at yours that we need."

The fact that Mum bought it and allowed me to leave with Daniel with zero protest made me realise how much she had warmed to him. Daniel took large strides up Kyle Road. I had to half run to keep up with him. He kept his head down and didn't talk all the way to his and I realised he was quite distressed.

It did seem a little disturbing uncovering the photograph. It opened up the possibility that Christian hadn't revealed a clear picture of the whole night if Daniel was unaware of his outfit change.

"What if the photo wasn't taken that night?" I said, as we marched up his drive. "It could've been a different Halloween."

"I'm pretty sure there's other people in front of him who were there that night. But that's partly what I want to check. I'm sure I've got a couple of other photos from the party stored in my folder."

We were greeted by loud opera singing as Daniel opened his front door. He rolled his eyes. "That's Dad's music. Just be thankful he's not singing along to it."

I felt a stab of melancholy at the memory of dad singing at the top of his voice whenever he cooked us breakfast in the kitchen. A wave of envy consumed me at the thought of Daniel getting to live here, with both of his parents every day, probably never even considering life could be any different.

As we stepped inside, I took in the large hallway.

It seemed to extend for miles. My trainers squeaked on the polished brown floorboards and I was careful not to stand on an expensive-looking burgundy rug with grey elephants embroidered round the edges. A vintage-style table to the right was adorned with two matching crystal vases, both overflowing with exotic flowers, the air heavy with their perfume. It was a very similar style of house to Patrick's, but the sophistication here was bathed in a homeliness.

"Come on." Daniel was climbing the stairs, two at a time. I started to follow just as a door to the left opened and a woman, who I presumed to be his mum (same black hair, tan skin and chiselled cheekbones), appeared holding a tray of cookies.

"Oh, hello." She looked momentarily baffled to see me, then smiled politely.

"Hi." I waved, glancing up at Daniel who had continued to the top of the stairs. He looked back, motioning for me to hurry up.

"Would you like a biscuit?" Daniel's mum held out the tray to me.

"Oh…" I hesitated, enticed by the sweet aroma.

"Mum, she doesn't want any biscuits," Daniel shouted in exasperation.

I frowned at his rudeness. "They look great, thanks." I took a couple off the tray and Daniel's mum beamed.

"I think 'she' has a name, Daniel," his mum shouted back at him. "What's your name, dear?"

"Darcy," I answered awkwardly, trying not to spray crumbs in her face.

Another flicker of bemusement. "Darcy. Well, that's a lovely name."

"Come on, Darcy," Daniel called.

"Thanks, bye." I hurried up the stairs, aware that

Mrs King was watching my every move.

"Sorry about that," Daniel said, leading me into his room.

I paused at the doorway, taking in the massive space. The distance between his bed and desk was practically larger than the whole breadth of our flat. A corner of the room had wall to wall bookcases, but it was the telescope set up at the bay window that caught my attention. "This is awesome." I strode over, marvelling at the white instrument.

"I've got it set up a certain way, so please don't adjust the magnification."

I laughed. "I never knew you could be so geeky."

He made a face as he fired up his laptop. I took a peek through the viewfinder, taking a while to angle myself properly. I smiled in wonder when a sprinkle of stars winked at me. Daniel's room backed onto the fields, so there were no streetlights tainting the view. My mind started to wander on an 'if only' trip... Now that Dad earned more he could have afforded to buy a house like this for us, as a family. I could have had a room that backed onto fields where I could stare at the stars all night long. Instead he had bought two flats – one for us and one for him, in London, with *her*.

I stepped away from the telescope and looked to a poster hanging on Daniel's wall. It was of a dark sky filled with millions of stars. It bore a quote in looping white letters: *We are made of Stardust*.

I watched as Daniel scrolled through his computer. "Daniel, do you know anyone at school called Edgar? I got this weird message earlier today…"

Daniel shook his head, engrossed in his searching. He called me over to the computer: "Here, this is

Christian in his pirate outfit."

I peered over his shoulder. "And what are you?"

"A mad scientist." Daniel's tone was defensive and I laughed.

He clicked through more photos. He stopped at one of a magician and a rabbit, then at another of a gangster dancing with witches. "Same outfits. This was definitely taken that night then. Why would Christian have changed? I don't get it." He forwarded through more pictures. A shot of a couple kissing caught my eye.

"Wait, go back," I instructed. I moved closer as the photograph opened again on the screen. The gangster was in the forefront of the shot, so I asked Daniel to zoom in, magnifying the couple. A tall boy, dressed in a surgeon's bloody gown with plastic gloves, kissing a girl in a cat outfit, blonde curls tied up in a bun.

"That's Patrick," Daniel said. "But it's not Louise he's kissing."

I shook my head. "No, it's Kara."

Post Murder: Scene Two

Christian could hear the malicious whispers from neighbours hissing up the street; they crept under his door at night and crawled into his nightmares. He was suspect number one. It felt like he was already on trial thanks to the village rumour mill working overtime.

His bedroom had become his sanctuary, the internet a window into the world he was no longer welcome in. It was frightening how many times his name was posted around various online platforms; strangers creating a distorted narrative of who he was and what happened the night of the party. He had to catch himself, thinking *'that poor guy'*, before realising the online Christian Henderson was him; that *he* was the poor victimised 'loner boy'.

One forum in particular was dominated by some guy called Edgar who seemed to think he knew Christian intimately. Christian felt a rage of anger every time he read any of Edgar's comments: *He often sat alone at break time, scribbling in that sketchbook of his, staring at Louise. He gave me the creeps. He used to cycle past her house late at night, staring in the windows.* What was this guy's deal? Did he think the forum was some kind of online game? It was his life these internet weirdos were messing with.

Christian scrolled through links to news stories and videos others had posted. A flash of shame scorched his cheeks as his mum's angry face filled the screen, her voice rising, silencing the chatter in the pub. The screen shook as the person filming adjusted their stance, capturing the audience of downcast faces, eyes refusing to make contact, the shaking of heads as his mum berated them. *"I know what you're all saying about my boy. My wean, a sixteen-year-old child. And you grown adults making him out to be some monster. You lot are the monsters. Aye, that's right you hang your head in shame, John Anderson. I heard your slanderous words on that news show. I bet it was your wee shite that threw the red paint over my car."* Christian closed the link, unable to watch as John Anderson's wife barrelled towards his mum, knowing what came next. The spilled beer, the tussle. He hated the thought of his mum ever finding this video, and the thought that everyone in the village had now probably seen it.

There was a soft knock on the door as it creaked open. Christian slammed his laptop shut. When his eyes met Daniel's, he swallowed back tears. Daniel had such a fierce look of loyalty on his face – as if he believed the sheer force of that alone could blow away the doubters and the haters.

"What you up to, man?" Daniel observed the heaped ashtray and muted television in the corner. He threw open the curtains, a slither of sunshine casting a beam of dust towards Christian. Christian held out his hand, imagining the beam could transport him to a parallel life where things hadn't gone so wrong.

Daniel lunged forward and grabbed his wrist. Christian blinked in surprise at the force of his grip. Anger sparked in Daniel's eyes and Christian pulled away his arm, rubbing at the red indents.

"What's with you?" Christian flicked off the television.

"Are you just going to hole up in here like you're guilty?" Daniel asked.

"It's not exactly Pleasantville out there. If the old

ladies aren't clucking at me then there's our stand-up classmates waiting to jump out at me with their phones, ready to document my every move for their online detective podcasts and forums."

He watched Daniel pace the room, kicking the end of his desk in frustration. "They're a bunch of ignorant, stuck-up pies. You're creating your own prison right here, man. I'm not leaving without you. We're going to head outside and you're going to hold your head up high because you're innocent."

A smile crept up Christian's face, then he chuckled.

Daniel folded his arms, defiant. "What's so funny?"

"*Pies*?" Christian shook his head.

Daniel huffed. "Well, I was trying to be polite. I can think of many other names I'd rather call them."

"Well, don't hold back on my account," Christian relented and scrambled forward, searching for his trainers. "I'll come out a quick bike ride with you."

Daniel's shoulders relaxed, as if he had been preparing for more of a fight.

As they descended the stairs, Christian's mum appeared from the kitchen, bloodshot eyes accentuated by her pale face. Without make-up, the lines on her face were more pronounced, and Christian couldn't shake the thought that every worry he caused her was scarring her face, etching deep.

When they spoke, Christian could feel guilt seeping deep down into his bones. He had stopped looking into her eyes, afraid of all of the emotions he would see tumbling from her. He'd heard her on the phone to his aunt the other night, giving him the answer as to why she'd stopped doing her holistic sessions at the local sports centre on Saturday mornings.

"Would you believe he actually asked me to leave? Billy Jones who I've known for ten years, telling me I'm upsetting the local regulars like I'm some god damn criminal. Where are these rumours coming from, Mary? It breaks my heart what they're saying about my boy."

"Where are you off to?" Her voice was quiet, desperate.

Daniel stepped forward. "We're just going a short bike ride, Mrs Henderson."

Christian's mum's face softened at Daniel's smile and she touched his arm. "Okay, son. You look after him, right?"

"Of course." Daniel squeezed her hand and from the whiteness of her knuckles Christian knew she was squeezing back a little too tightly.

Christian opened the front door, closing his eyes, enjoying the sensation of air in his lungs. Daniel was right – his room was becoming a prison and that was a stupid thing to allow. Just in case…

As they sped through the streets to the bike track, Christian felt all of his tension unfurl as his muscles pumped through the anger and helplessness.

His phone vibrated in his pocket and he knew who it would be. He tried to block all thoughts from his head, still unsure how the conversation might play out. The phone calls kept coming in from withheld numbers. Was it so there would be no trace of number logs on his phone?

Words from their conversations wound through his head and the niggling that he could fill in blanks that no one knew, talk more to the police, were buried every time a call came in. *We can't tell.*

As Christian tailed Daniel through the woods the

wind ripped against his face. Freedom. It was a word he had never paid much attention to before, a concept he had always taken for granted. He had been free to choose anything, be anything, his whole life in front of him.

As the descent steepened, he felt the dip in his stomach. It was as if he was falling, but with the thrill of knowing the sensation was momentary.

Right now, sailing down the hill, he still had time to choose the story's ending.

Chapter Fourteen

Dear Darcy,

Thanks for your letter, even if I did need to read it twice over because of your messy handwriting.

So, your mum is dating Mr Harris? He's a decent guy – one of the good ones. He was very protective of my mum throughout my trial, and for that I'll be forever grateful – he helped to keep her sane. I feel bad that they're not together anymore. But it got complicated.

Do you get on well with your mum? Do you still see your dad?

My dad has started to write to me in here. The worst part is I know he believes I actually did murder Louise. His letters are heavy with guilt, like he thinks because he left us I turned into this out-of-control murderer. I can sense it in his tone, like he wants to help me become a better person or something – he tells me to take every course possible in here, to read about Buddhism, to cleanse my soul, whatever.

At first, I think Mum thought I was guilty too. The worst day was when the police arrested me and took me down to the station. Daniel had persuaded me to go a bike ride earlier that day, like he had a sixth sense, knowing those would be my last hours of freedom. When I saw the flicker of doubt and fear in Mum's eyes when the police read me my rights, I was terrified. If my own mum thought I was guilty, what hope did I have?

I don't think I've ever been so scared, walking into the police station. One of the policemen interviewing me – let's call him McDuff – was so off with me the moment I sat down, and I knew then I was screwed.

Every time I tried to answer his questions, this taunting voice, *He thinks you did it,* kept pounding in my head, clouding my thoughts.

McDuff's opening line was that I was being charged with possession of a knife. At first I was relieved; that was way better than being charged with murder, right? I'd been stupid, thinking it was okay to wear a knife if it was part of a Halloween costume. He lured me into a false sense of hope – that I would be getting off with a caution.

Then McDuff laid the knife on the table – it was bagged with a label: 'Exhibit A: Murder Weapon'. He left that sitting right in front of me as he continued with his questioning. I couldn't even look at Mum's face. I could feel her knee trembling beside me and I think I felt worse about that, knowing I was upsetting her. McDuff told me that my fingerprints were the only 'positive match' and all I could think was, *How could any of this be positive?* I wanted to scream it right in his arrogant, slimy face.

Then the other policeman slammed my lost bag down on the table, telling me I'd left the party so quickly I'd forgotten it, but someone had helpfully handed it in to the station. McDuff then slid a book across the table to me – my sketchbook. "Open it," he said. I will never forget the look on my mum's face when I turned the pages, revealing images of Louise – sketches I had penned of her daydreaming in class, running during cross-country. I knew how it looked. I tried to explain to them that I liked sketching people, that I thought Louise had an interesting face.

Of course, McDuff made a big deal about how beautiful Louise was, how I clearly had a crush on her, maybe even a little obsession? How many sketches were in that book? Seven, maybe ten?

It felt like I was having an out-of-body experience in that room. I don't think I've ever felt so helpless, trying to argue my innocence to people who had clearly already decided my guilt. That room was heavy with anger. Rowantree is such a small tight-knit community people felt connected to Louise even if they'd never met her.

It's a posh village and I was the boy who didn't fit, a demon who needed to be caught before the place was tainted with my evil. I had never fully understood the danger of being the weirdo outside family until that moment. The Marshalls were so popular and well-known. I'm pretty sure right from the start they hated the thought of me being anywhere near their daughter that night and that they had already decided it was me. Other parents were terrified it could be their girl next. It caused irrational panic and anger.

I was convinced that day that Mum thought I was guilty. She maybe still does, but at some point she clearly decided that didn't matter, she loved me so much that she was going to fight for me. That's what I struggle with the most. Knowing Mum is still fighting for my release. But she's really strong. I know she can cope with it. My dad isn't so strong. But he has another family now to support him.

I'm quite jealous of your outdoor exploits. I get some outside time here, but it's not the same – it always feels claustrophobic in here. Sometimes I have dreams where I'm flying over mountains – those are my favourites. For a few seconds when I wake up I have that sense of feeling free – of being out in the open, breathing in real air.

What are your thoughts of the Bratz then? (Patrick, Kara, and Zoe). D'you think Zoe's coping ok since her mum died?

And how is Daniel? Is he still a big nerd? Sorry this has been a big outpouring of one of the worst days of my life, but I've actually found it quite therapeutic reliving the trauma.

Later,

Christian Henderson

Dear Christian,

Seeing as you find my handwriting so hard to read, I thought I'd make things easier for you and return to email. And also it's quicker.

I don't even know where to start in response to your last letter. I can't even imagine how horrific that must have been, finding yourself being interrogated like that, feeling so helpless. When I met your mum she was 100% on your side, Christian. Truly, it was clear to me that she thinks you're innocent. I'm sure she was just shocked that day, like you were.

There's something I need to ask you – Daniel said we should just drop things and leave it be, but I know it's truly bothering him. We found a photo of you at Louise's Halloween party and you're not in your pirate costume – you're wearing some kind of white sheet. Did you go back to the party later on? Also, we found a photo of Patrick kissing Kara. What if Louise found them together that night and that had something to do with what happened?

I'm glad you think Mr Harris is a decent guy. I do too. Kara said something about him recently (which Zoe dismissed). It unnerved me but I reckon it was just a stupid rumour...

I think Zoe gets sad sometimes but seems to be coping ok. Kara and Patrick seem pretty protective of her, which is nice. What was wrong with her mum? I know she was ill for some time, but I don't like to ask Zoe about it.

I do get on really well with Mum, most of the time. She's a bit nuts, but lots of fun. Sometimes I feel like I'm the one looking after her – she can be so flaky. My dad...I haven't really spoken to him much since he moved to London. I'm still angry with him. But I guess I can see Mum is a bit happier again now, so that means they probably weren't meant to be together. She told me, when he first left, that it's always easier to blame the one who runs away. I think that was her way of trying to explain to me that she wasn't perfect either. I already know that...it just feels like he ran away from me too. I mean, why couldn't he have taken a promotion a bit closer to home? He was never really good at opening up to me, and I feel like maybe if he'd sat me down properly and explained things a bit better it might have hurt less.

Did you ever think that your dad maybe just feels guilty in general? That doesn't mean that he has doubts about your innocence. It sounds to me like he just wants you to know that he's looking out for you, that he's concerned that prison life will rot your brain. Which is partly why I'm bothering you too – you know, just to keep you connected to an intellectual realm of the world.

Truly, it sounds like both of your parents are on your side, and believe in you. I think you need to hold on to that sense of hope – that people are rooting for you.

Daniel is still a nerd, yes. I can tell he misses you a lot.

Later,

Darcy x

Dear Darcy,

I think I underestimated your super sleuth capabilities. How did you manage to find a photo that was missed by the social-media witch hunters?

I think this one deserves a face to face explanation. How would you and Daniel like to pay me a visit?

Christian

Chapter Fifteen

Christian's letter fluttered out of my hand as I picked up my phone to call Daniel.

"Yo, what's happening?" I could hear the sounds of screeching cars in the background and I pictured Daniel on his play station.

"I got another letter from Christian. He wants us to visit him." My hands started to sweat as I paced up and down my bedroom.

Silence.

"Hello? Did you hear me?"

"I'm just surprised. He never wants me to visit. Maybe he's curious about meeting you."

"Well, it might have something to do with a question I asked…"

"What question?" Daniel sounded wary.

"Well, I maybe asked him about the photo we found."

"Darcy, we agreed to drop it." Daniel sighed. *"I don't know why you went ahead and asked about it when you said you wouldn't. It's a bit weird how obsessed you are with all of this."*

I blinked, stung by Daniel's bluntness. Maybe I was pushing things too much, but Christian's letter about the day of his arrest had affected me. It made me think more than ever that he was innocent. "Don't you want to know the truth?" I pressed, an answer forming in my head as soon as I asked: *Not if he's guilty.* Perhaps that was why Daniel was so reluctant to question Christian - he was scared of the answer. I waited for Daniel to respond.

"Okay, we should go. It's the October holiday next week, so how about one of those days?"

I thought back to the conversations Zoe and Kara had been having at school the past couple of weeks, their persuasive skills nearly convincing me to join them at the cabin. I hadn't committed either way. I had turned down Dad's invitation a few days ago and still felt a horrible gnaw of guilt when I thought back to the disappointment I'd heard in his voice. I'd promised I would see him during the Christmas holidays.

"We should try to arrange the start of the week," I suggested.

"Okay, leave it to me. I'm guessing Christian must be planning to call me this evening, as he needs to set it up. I'll let you know what we agree."

"Okay, cool, thanks. See you tomorrow at school." When I hung up my hands were shaking, a flash of fear and excitement rushing through my body. I was going to hear his voice; sit in front of him and look into his eyes.

I was going to meet Christian Henderson.

*

One week today. It was all I could think about. I kept waking in the middle of the night, mind racing over extracts of Christian's case, sometimes getting out the case files, scribbling diagrams, trying to connect names, clues. The words from his letters bled into my dreams when I did sleep. I imagined what we might say to each other, pictured the expression on his face as we said hello for the first time. Would he still resemble the haunted boy in the photographs?

As I got dressed for school, Mum poked her head round the door.

"Did I see your light on when I got up during the

night?"

I slammed the wardrobe shut, hiding a string of post-it notes that I had pinned up inside the door, documenting any new 'evidence' I came across about Christian's case.

"I was having trouble sleeping, so I read for a bit." I inadvertently looked towards my jewellery box, my hiding place for Christian's letters. Mum would flip if she knew what I had been reading last night.

Mum opened my door wider. "Everything okay at school?"

I ordered my brain to settle and managed to flash what I hoped was a care-free smile. "As okay as school can be."

"Good." Mum hesitated and I tried to read her expression, but she shot me a dazzling smile of her own. "See you later, sweetie."

*

As I walked through the corridors at school, I tried to find traces of Christian in the artwork displayed in Mr Harris's room, searching for his scrawl amongst graffiti on walls, on desks. Weirdly, the desk I had on my first day in English – the one with *Christian* indented into the wood - had disappeared. I needed a sign to reassure me the visit was a good idea - that I hadn't lost my mind.

I glanced around the classroom, scanning desks. The room started to fill up. I needed to find his name.

"Where are you going?" Daniel frowned as I gathered up my books.

"My chair's wobbly." I tried not to look too obvious as I stared at desks on my way to the back of the classroom. *Christian, Christian, Christian.* His name circled my head as I sought out his graffiti. A wave of relief crashed over me as I spotted it, two desks from the back, beside Zoe.

"Can I help you?" A girl I had never spoken to was edging into the seat at the desk. I refused to move, making it impossible for her to get past.

Zoe shot me a curious look and I grinned. "I was hoping to sit with you today, if that's okay?"

Zoe shrugged, bemused. "Sure." She smiled up at the girl. "Sorry, Tara."

"Seriously?" Tara huffed loudly, cursing under her breath as she made her way to another desk. I slid into the seat, my fingers tracing Christian's name. I kept my head down, avoiding Daniel's attempt to catch my eye.

"Everything okay?" Zoe looked from Daniel to me.

"Uh, yeah." I placed my book on top of Christian's name. "I just didn't want to get hassled today. Mrs Clark always picks on people at the front."

Zoe made a face in agreement. I looked at the paper in front of her, noticing it was a hand-written letter. She slid it between the pages of her notebook, turning her attention to Mrs Clark.

Mrs Clark clapped her hands, asking for silence. "Okay, so today I thought we could do something a bit different and focus on something at least one of you has asked for more of. We're going to be looking at gothic poets."

A spatter of groans circled the room.

"Who asked for *that*?" Patrick shot a disparaging look around his classmates.

The noise faded to background and my body relaxed. I felt reassured that I had found Christian's name. I took it as a sign that the visit would be okay.

Mrs Clark started to hand out photocopies of poetry. I read the titles: *The Raven* and *The Bells*, both by Edgar Allan Poe.

"*The Raven* is arguably one of his most recognised poems, I always think it sounds best read aloud. I'll read the first verse then I'll get one of you to take over."

As Mrs Clark started to recite a haunting verse, the name Edgar jumped out at me. There had been no other messages, so I hadn't given the name much thought again. But now, seeing it written down, I realised I had seen it before, somewhere else. *Think, think.*

I glanced at Zoe's paper. She was doodling roses around the poetry stanzas. I wondered if someone called Edgar attended our school. I was about to ask her, when Mrs Clark strode past, annunciating words in a dramatic voice, *"As of some one gently rapping, rapping at my chamber door…"* Zoe was engrossed in Mrs Clark's performance. I decided I could ask Daniel at lunchtime.

*

Daniel was up and out the door as soon as the bell rang. I chased him halfway down the corridor before he told me he was ditching me in favour of going to a computer games discussion group. I couldn't blame him, after my weirdness in class. I was secretly pleased that it might give me a chance to sit with Kara, Zoe and Patrick. When I arrived in the canteen, I scanned the tables and queues and finally spotted Zoe sitting on a bench in the back corner, a book in one hand, a sandwich in the other. Roo sat next to her, scrolling through her phone. No Patrick or Kara.

I hesitated, deliberating about joining them. There was something intimidating about Roo. Before I could turn away, Roo suddenly looked up, eyes locking with mine. She shot me a curious look and I wandered over. "Hey. Mind if I sit? Sorry, I promise I'm not stalking you." I directed that comment at Zoe, my casual tone a contradiction to the nerves tumbling inside of me.

Zoe looked up, clearly surprised to see me again, then nudged Roo, telling her to scoot over so I could sit down.

"One sec. I'm at a really good bit," Zoe murmured, turning the page of her book.

I pulled out my lunch, glancing at the title – some horror. I noted the chipped black nail varnish on Zoe's nails, thinking it was an appropriate match. Her Art folder was propped against her knees and my eyes traced the outline of a crow - very similar to the tattoo on her back - its beak tapping against a door covered in red roses.

"Soo, Darcy. What do you think of Rowantree so far?"

Roo's knee knocked against mine, her closeness making me feel uneasy. Her hair smelled of marshmallows, and the mint from her chewing gum wafted towards me.

I shrugged. "It's nice."

Roo guffawed. "Where are you from anyways? Zoe here says you're quite fascinated by our little murder village." Zoe's head snapped up at that but she didn't say anything. Roo continued, "I bet you OD on True Crime documentaries and podcasts. They always have a way of putting a glamourous spin on stuff, sensationalising the victim and all that. There's nothing f'ing glamourous about murder though."

There was a challenge in her eyes, like she wanted me to argue something different. I swallowed a bite of my sandwich, not sure how to respond.

Roo continued, "Everyone is always interested

when a beautiful girl dies, don't you think? That really helps with the glamour, when there's a beautiful dead face smiling out from the papers. And everyone conveniently forgets what an actual stuck-up horror she was in real life."

"Roo," Zoe slammed her book shut. "Can you go now and find your friends?"

Roo rolled her eyes and jumped up from the bench, saluting her sister. "Aye, aye, sister. Catch you later, Darcy."

I mumbled a 'bye, relieved when Roo disappeared into the crowds.

Zoe sighed, "Sorry, my sister can be a bit ...dramatic. What's new with you?" She gave me her full attention.

"Not much," I shrugged, desperately wanting to tell her about the arranged visit to see Christian. "Where are Patrick and Kara?"

She made a face. "Last I saw of them they were holding hands and heading to the sheds."

It struck me that I rarely saw Patrick and Kara apart. Always walking hand and hand through the corridors, sitting together at breaks, on the bus home. I studied the drawn look on Zoe's face, wondering if she sometimes felt like a third wheel.

"They seem pretty close," I commented, wanting to see how she would react.

Zoe shrugged. "Patrick has been a big support to her. He was to me too, when my mum...got really bad."

Like one big happy family. Her words from the other week came back to me. I wondered what it had been like when Louise was in the mix; how she would have reacted if she'd caught Patrick and Kara kissing at her party. From Kara's stories the night we were in the hills, I guessed Louise would not have taken it well.

"I'm sorry about your mum. It must be really hard," I said.

"Yeah." Zoe nodded. "She had cancer and was ill for a long time with it, but it still came as a shock, you know, having to say goodbye." Zoe's knuckles whitened as she gripped her book. "I worry about Roo too. She acts really brazen and confident but she's a mess. I feel like I need to be a mum to her, but I don't know how to handle her sometimes. It's exhausting."

I wanted to tell Zoe that Roo was so lucky to have a sister looking out for her, but I worried it would sound too cheesy. I reached into my bag and pulled out a chocolate bar.

"Here, I reserve this for emergencies - usually double period Maths, but I think you should have it."

Zoe smiled and slipped it into her coat pocket. "Thanks, Darcy."

I drummed my fingers against the bench, debating if I could trust Zoe. I wasn't going to get closer to answers if I didn't ask questions.

"I found out something the other day..." I started. Zoe's head jerked up, a flash of something in her eyes. *Panic?*

She held my gaze, waiting for me to continue.

"Were Patrick and Kara seeing each other behind Louise's back?"

"Who told you that? Kara?"

I shook my head. "It doesn't matter. Did Louise know about it?"

Zoe nodded. "She found out. Not much got past Louise."

"How did she react?"

Zoe hesitated, like her doubts mirrored mine;

could she trust me? "She didn't let on for weeks. I thought she was oblivious, but in true Louise style she decided to play games, ramping up her public shows of affection with Patrick in front of Kara. And she kept making little comments to Kara, like if she ate any more chocolate she might not find a boyfriend as she was getting fat. And she started to share quite embarrassing personal stories about Kara when we were all together."

"How did Kara react?" I couldn't imagine her tolerating that kind of behaviour for long.

"She was very quiet at first, which made me suspicious. Usually, Kara would have given as good as she got. And then she did, that night at the Halloween party. She got pretty drunk and started to get quite handsy with Patrick in front of lots of people."

"Including Louise?"

Zoe looked like she was going to continue with her story, then stopped. "Why are you so curious about all of this, about all of us?"

My face flushed. "Sorry, I didn't mean to be so nosy."

"It's fine. But you need to remember Louise's death upset a lot of people. Kara doesn't like talking about her. We all just want to forget that night. People did things they regretted...so of course there's going to be unanswered questions."

Like what? I wanted to ask, but that would be pushing my luck.

Zoe must have sensed my desperate curiosity. She picked at a loose thread on her skirt, a nervous gesture. There was a silence and I waited, wondering if Zoe would fill it. "Let's just say there were a lot of arguments that night, fuelled with too much alcohol."

I sat forward, trying to figure out if Zoe was trying to give me a clue without actually saying anything. Did Louise confront Kara and Patrick that night? Did Kara snap? Or Patrick?

The bell rang just as other questions were forming in my head. Zoe grabbed her stuff, jumping up. "I have to get going, I'm at the other end of the school next period. Catch you later."

I hadn't even formed a goodbye when she disappeared into the crowds, leaving behind a trail of question marks.

Chapter Sixteen

The train felt stuffy and claustrophobic. I opened the window a crack, straightening my skirt for the fifth time, sitting back down on my hands, trying to stop fidgeting.

"Jesus, if I knew you were going to be this nervous I would have brought a supply of my mum's Valium and popped it in your lemonade."

"Your mum takes Valium?" I looked at Daniel curiously.

He sighed and went back to playing some game on his phone. I stared out the window, trying to lull myself into a hypnotic state by tracing the miles and miles of hay bales along the fields.

I looked at my watch, dismayed that only ten minutes had passed.

"What if he changes his mind when we get there, and they turn us away, saying that he doesn't want any visitors?"

Daniel didn't even look up from his phone, just shook his head.

On my own phone was a message from Mum:

Have a great time x

A flash of guilt washed over me. I had created a story that me and Daniel were visiting one of his cousins in another town. If I had said we were going to the cinema, or anywhere remotely interesting, she would have demanded to hear plotlines and see photos. I knew she had taken a sneaky afternoon off work to spend time with Mr Harris as he was also off on the school October break. Hopefully she would be too doe-eyed to quiz me too much about the 'cousin' when I returned. Daniel had agreed we should go out for dinner after visiting Christian to make our trip seem longer and more authentic.

I wondered what Christian would say about the photograph. Daniel looked surprisingly nonchalant about the whole visit, but I knew a part of him must be on tenterhooks too, wondering what explanation Christian might have. Would it lead to conflict?

What if Daniel stormed out, leaving me alone with Christian? Or, worse still, kicked off so much that they detained him, leaving me to try to explain to both Mum and the Kings why Daniel had come to be in a young offenders' unit.

A message popped up on my phone. A chill ran up my legs when the words connected:

PRIVATE MESSAGE to Darcy Thomas
From: Edgar
Sometimes when you dig for the truth, you don't find the answers you want to hear. Do yourself a favour and stop snooping. This is your second friendly warning. Next time, I won't be so friendly.

I looked over at Daniel, who was still engrossed with whatever game he was playing. I waved a hand in front of his face, thrusting the message above his phone.

"Look at this. Who is this Edgar?"

He read the message briefly, his expression neutral. "Looks like some idiot just playing around."

I shook my head. "No, it's more than that. Is there anyone called Edgar in our year?"

Daniel frowned. "The name does seem kind of familiar, actually. I think he posted on some of the forums."

"I knew I'd seen that name before! But how would he know who I am? We should go back over his postings – they might give us a clue about his identity."

I turned back to my phone, looking up the links I'd saved when I'd read over Daniel's shoulder.

Daniel sighed. "Can we not do this just now? We're nearly there."

Our stop came into view. I slid my phone into my bag, vowing to go back to it on the way home. I shivered at the thought of this Edgar keeping tracks on me.

The rain started lashing down just as we stepped onto the platform. The station was so small there was no waiting room, so we huddled in a shelter, the rain ricocheting off the plastic roof – *bang bang bang*, in time with my heart.

"Have you got the number of the taxi company?" I asked Daniel, just as he started to speak to an operator. I was glad he was with me. As I watched him speak confidently into the phone, I decided that Daniel would be top of my list of people to be stuck with if I were ever to be in a crisis.

I pulled my jacket tighter around me, wishing for the thousandth time that I hadn't worn my Smashing Pumpkins t-shirt. It was cringe and would make me look desperate to connect with Christian.

Mum had approved, not realising my motivations of course. She grinned as she ran to her bedroom, upturning an old suitcase she was yet to unpack, running into the living room swinging around her Cherub Rock t-shirt and pulling it on over her dress.

We both tried not to notice how tight it was across her bust and waist.

I buttoned my jacket up to my neck, deciding that I would keep it hidden for the duration of the visit.

The taxi arrived and I let Daniel do the talking. The driver thankfully didn't attempt polite conversation or ask who we might be visiting. I did see him glance at my bag a couple of times through the mirror, maybe wondering if young people who went on visits to the offenders' unit were the kind who would do him out of a fare.

My tongue stuck to the roof of my mouth as the taxi swung round a corner and the offenders' unit came into view. I tried to imagine how Christian must have felt the day he was driven here, knowing he was being put away for many years. Did he arrive in a police van? Was he handcuffed? These were all questions I wanted to ask him, but they seemed far too intrusive.

We climbed out of the taxi and stood at the gates, my hands shaking as I put up my umbrella. Daniel stooped to fit under it with me and I raised my arm so that I didn't decapitate him. Our eyes locked. We didn't need to say anything to understand how each other felt. I hesitated, then slowly slid my hand into his and gave a reassuring squeeze. He squeezed back and we started towards the main entrance.

We had to sign in at the front desk area, handing over our ID to be checked. As we walked through the metal detectors I felt like a criminal and started to sweat, even though I had nothing to feel guilty about. Daniel had warned me that sometimes Dog Unit officers patrolled, but there was no sign of them today.

We were patted down and my bag was searched

before we were allowed upstairs and through to the main hall. There were so many people milling about that it felt a bit like walking into the school canteen, only the seats looked more comfortable. One of the guards showed us to a table near the back corner, the empty chair across from ours blinking at me like a neon light, '*This is Christian's seat. In a few minutes he is going to be sitting across from you, talking to you, looking into your eyes.*'

As I sat down I tried not to stare at the other visitors and the 'prisoners' being led out. Most had swaggers and skinheads and an air of aggressive bravado that put me on edge. A couple of boys glanced in my direction, and I sank further down into my chair, hoping Daniel's frame would block me from view.

He touched my arm, sitting up. "There he is."

Heart hammering, I looked up just as a pair of piercing blue eyes met mine. His hair was shorter, the blonde streaks stark against the greasy mess of brown underneath. Stubble sprinkled his jaw, and his cheekbones were more pronounced, reminding me he was now older than the boy in the photographs. His stride was slow, with a lilt of melancholy, like the joy had been drained from him. The goose bumps darting up my arms were telling me he was even better looking than I had imagined.

"Hey, man." Christian high fived Daniel, who grinned, slapping his hand with exuberance.

Christian's voice was deep, almost gravelly, again making him seem older.

"Hey, dude. How you doing?"

Christian half smiled. "I've stayed in better hotels, but one can't complain."

I held my breath as Christian turned his attention

to me. I could feel a flush creeping up my neck and I attempted a casual smile.

"Hi, Christian."

"Hello, Darcy." His eyes smiled. "We meet at last."

We sat looking at each other for a moment, and I wished I had left my jacket unbuttoned after all – so he could see my t-shirt. *Take it off*, a little voice inside my head said, but then the shy, awkward me won out and instead I turned to look at Daniel, who was talking a hundred words a minute.

Christian laughed from time to time as Daniel filled him in on his news, but it sounded hollow and strained. Christian's eyes darted to other prisoners, his leg jangling under the table. I wondered if some of them bullied him? I shivered at the thought.

His eyes met mine again and my mind jolted, thoughts and words tumbling silently in no coherent order.

"So, Darcy the detective. How's your work on my case going?"

I opened and closed my mouth, cheeks flaming.

He chuckled. "Don't look so flummoxed, I'm just teasing. But really, ten out of ten for finding that photo of me at the party. Can I ask where you saw it? Some internet podcast?"

I hesitated, glancing at Daniel.

"She found it in a box belonging to Patrick," Daniel said, his face now serious. "I thought it must have been from another year, a different party, but other people who were there that night were in the photo. You were in a blood-stained white sheet and that ties up with postings from people who said they saw you walking around in ripped white clothes, as a ghost."

I watched Christian's expression intently, looking for signs of panic, but his face was patient and measured, like he was listening carefully and with interest to Daniel.

"It was taken that night," Christian confirmed.

"So, you went back? Or you changed outfits halfway through the night? I don't get it." Daniel frowned, shaking his head.

"I went back," Christian said.

"Why?"

"I left my lighter behind. You know how important that lighter is to me."

Daniel nodded. "Yeah, I know it's your dad's. But why did you change your outfit? What happened?"

"Someone puked on my pirate outfit, so I shoved that in the machine at home and went back to the party in my jeans and t-shirt. People were pretty drunk as it was getting late – I think you must have gone home, I couldn't find you. There was this girl, Hayley, some fashion-design college student who was friends with Kara and Zoe. She kept following me round with an old sheet, telling me I had to have a Halloween costume and she was going to make me one. I just wanted to get her out of my way so I could find my lighter, so I let her dress me in the sheet. Was she in the photo?"

Daniel looked to me for clarification.

"No," I answered. "Unless she was a rabbit or a gangster."

Christian grinned at Daniel. "Shame, she was pretty hot. Totally your type, Daniel."

Daniel's face flamed. I wondered what his type was.

"Anyway, she really went to town, slicing up the sheet, painting my face, throwing fake blood over me, the lot."

I could see Daniel's frown lines deepen. "Why didn't you tell the police you went back? You said you'd gone straight to bed when you went home."

Christian shrugged. "I didn't want to give them any more reason to try and pin it on me. You've got no idea, man, with the police. One guy wanted to get me from the beginning, regardless of what story I tried to tell him."

Story. The word jumped out at me. Stories were fiction, could twist the truth.

Daniel sighed. "I know, man. I know."

Christian raised an eyebrow at me. "Does that satisfy your curiosity, Darcy?"

I shrugged. "I guess. Did you find your lighter then?"

"I did." Christian nodded.

"Where did you leave it?" I asked.

Christian cracked a smile. "You'd make a good police officer. I found it upstairs in Louise's parents' bedroom, where I left it."

"Was Louise still there?"

Christian paused. "No, Darcy."

A horrible thought struck me. What if she had been out on the balcony already, dead, when Christian had slipped into the room for his lighter?

Christian looked away, his face paling. I wondered if a similar thought had crossed his mind.

There was an uncomfortable silence, then Christian surprised us by mentioning that his mum had visited recently.

"She said she'd met you, Darcy, and that you wanted to solve my case."

I started to explain but Christian continued, "She's been putting so much energy into her Justice campaign and I know she isn't getting anywhere, but she seemed to have some renewed desperate hope after she met you. I think it's a false hope, Darcy. Don't you? I just can't stand the thought of someone giving her more false hope."

I struggled to know how to answer. Christian hadn't mentioned any of this in his letters, maybe because he didn't know how to confront me about it.

"I'm sorry, I didn't mean to put your mum through any more pain. I've not seen her or been in touch with her since."

"Yeah, we just bumped into her, Christian. She just seemed pleased we were both rooting for you."

"I know." Christian shrugged, like he was relenting. "I do appreciate your support. It means a lot. I just don't want Mum wasting her whole life fighting for me, y'know?"

We nodded, another awkward silence stretching out in front of us.

Daniel changed the subject, asking Christian how he was getting on. Christian gave very general updates, talking about some classes in art and creative writing that he was taking. I started to understand why he discouraged visitors – the conversation was stilted. There was the glaring fact that Daniel and I were studying courses too, with the intention to go to Uni or find jobs. For Christian, classes seemed to be serving the purpose of simply keeping his mind stimulated – of preventing him going insane.

I was disappointed that Christian's conversation switched back to small talk. I was so used to his letters referring to other aspects of his life, that it almost felt like a different person was in front of me. I resisted referencing any parts of our written conversation and kept my chat light too.

When it came to leave, the disappointment on Daniel's face mirrored my own. After so much anticipation, the visit was over.

We stood up and I watched awkwardly as Daniel embraced Christian in a tight hug, the guard nearest us watching intently, as if Daniel was trying to pass on something illegal. To my surprise, Christian stooped down and hugged me too, not so tight, but still enough to send my heart racing.

"It was nice to meet you, Darcy," he whispered in my ear, stubble scratching against my cheek. I tried to return the sentiment, but the words didn't quite make it out my mouth.

Daniel and I turned to leave just as another boy walked past us. He paused to look me up and down, a leer on his face, and I instinctively stepped back.

"Hey, Henderson," the boy shouted to Christian's retreating back. "This one isn't as hot as your other schoolgirl. When's she coming back?"

Christian's shoulders tensed but he didn't turn around, instead giving his tormentor the finger.

Daniel grabbed my arm protectively, ushering me forward. I could feel my cheeks burning, but curiosity was winning over any feelings of embarrassment.

I wanted to shout after them: *What girl?*

Chapter Seventeen

A sense of relief flooded through me as we exited the unit. I had to resist the urge to run through the gates and to keep running until the looming grey building was simply a dot on the horizon.

"That was pretty intense," I puffed, realising I had been holding my breath. Daniel looked at his feet as he walked, hands stuffed into his pockets.

"So, should we call a taxi to get us back into the town centre and find somewhere to have a snack?" I checked the time. It was only four. "We could even go to the cinema first if you want."

Daniel didn't look up. "I'm not hungry."

He kept walking and I followed. The sun was piercing the sky, warming the damp air. Daniel seemed to be wandering aimlessly.

"Are we heading in the right direction for town?" I asked cautiously.

"Do you mind if we just head back to the station? I think I'd rather just get home."

"Oh, okay." I was disappointed that he didn't seem to want to analyse the visit. "Are we just walking then?"

He shrugged. "It's a nice day now. It shouldn't take us too long."

*

I managed to keep quiet on the walk back and as soon as we were on the train Daniel plugged in his ear buds and shut his eyes, signalling he wasn't in the mood for chatting yet. I opened the forum links I'd saved and managed to find a thread debating aspects of Christian's innocence, or in most cases, his guilt. I clicked on some comments responding to the headline: *She's only pretty when she doesn't talk...*

I scanned down the list, eyes drawn to postings from 'Edgar'. He had logged in to the forums; a lot. Edgar claimed to have been there the night of the party, and said he had found Christian's bag containing his sketchbook and handed it in at the police station.

That guy definitely had a thing for Louise. He was always watching her in class at school, scribbling away in his sketchbook. He never talked to her though, just gave her creepy looks from afar. I don't think she even noticed.

I scrolled through some more vulgar comments from guys - along the lines of: they knew what they would have given her.

I found other comments from Edgar under further postings about Christian's costume that night:

I saw him later that night, running down the stairs. He was wearing white sheets, the shredded parts wound round his legs, nearly tripping him up. There was blood down the fronts of the sheets, some looked fake, like it was too bright a shade of red. But I saw darker drops further down the sheets, like real blood had definitely seeped into them.

Star: *Hey, I was at the party too and I didn't know this guy but I remember seeing him there. I commented to my friend that he looked totally spooked, and I'm sure I saw blood on his hands. I remember saying it looked real. I'm sure I actually said, 'Like he had just killed someone'. It sends shivers through me just typing these words.*

User1111: *So, did the police find that costume? Why was there no mention of this anywhere else?*

Edgar: *A few of us mentioned it to the police. I don't know if they followed it up.*

GothGirl: *There was a bonfire burning in the park that night – some of the people from the party were there in the early hours. I reckon he stopped off there on his way home and burnt this outfit.*

Star: *Surely someone would have seen him throwing sheets into the fire?*

User 1111: *Not if it was really late. His Mum wasn't home that night, was she? So, he could have been out all night and no one would have known. Did the police analyse the bonfire?*

Edgar: *I don't know who you are, GothGirl, but there was no bonfire in the park that night.*

Daniel: *You're all of a bunch of losers. There was no other outfit. He was dressed as a pirate. I live in Rowantree and didn't see any bonfire in the park that night either. Go and find something else to amuse your pathetic little lives.*

I smirked and smiled over at Daniel. His eyes were now open, so I put my phone away and waved a hand in front of his face.

"Hey, you okay?" I asked.

He took out one of his earbuds and took so long to

respond that I thought he was going to ignore me.

"It's depressing seeing him in there. I always hate leaving. It makes me feel guilty, like I keep walking away and can't do anything."

I nodded, understanding completely. I held up my phone. "I just came across one of your postings on a forum, sticking up for him. So it's not like you didn't, or don't, do anything."

Daniel shrugged.

"That Edgar guy, he did post lots on the forums. It looked like he wanted Christian to be found guilty. And now he's messaging me – it has to be someone who knows I've been in touch with Christian and doesn't like it."

Daniel nodded but didn't really seem to be listening, like something else was bothering him. Maybe Christian's explanation for returning to the party. It had felt a bit convoluted to me. And was he wondering about the reference to the schoolgirl too?

The words were tumbling out before I could stop them, "Who else do you think has been visiting him?"

Daniel frowned. "What do you mean?"

"That guy, saying I wasn't as hot as the other girl who visits," I said.

"Oh, that." Daniel was dismissive. "He was just being an arse, trying to wind Christian up. I bet it was a stupid reference to his mum."

I sat back. I hadn't thought about that. Boys could be totally immature like that. But would he really have referred to Christian's mum as a *school*girl? It implied that someone had shown up wearing school uniform.

"Or it wouldn't surprise me if Christian's 'stalker letter writers' all visit him in there. That would not surprise me one bit." Daniel rolled his eyes and my face flushed.

Could I be perceived in the same way?

Would Christian let them visit him? He was probably so bored in there that it could be an easy form of entertainment.

*

When we arrived back in Rowantree it wasn't even six. I half hoped Daniel would invite me over to his, not feeling in the mood to return to an empty flat to cook dinner, certain that Mum would still be out with Mr Harris. I hadn't even bothered to text her to let her know I was on my way home. She wasn't expecting me back till much later and I didn't want her to think she had to cut short her date. Daniel barely said goodbye and I sighed, watching his retreating back as he ran up the hill. As I approached Kyle Road, I noticed a tall male leaning against a tree, talking on his phone. When he moved, the streetlight caught his face and I realised it was Patrick. Why wasn't he at the cabin? They should have left by now. He ended his call and slumped back against the tree, shoulders visibly shaking. Was he crying?

I hesitated, not wanting him to realise I'd seen him, but there was no other route to get to my flat complex. I slowed, trying my best to creep past. My boot caught on the kerb and I stumbled. The noise startled Patrick.

He immediately straightened, wiping at his eyes, smoothing his hair back from his face. "Hey, Darcy, what's up?" His breezy tone sounded forced and his swagger had no conviction as he headed towards me.

"Not much. What you up to?" Up close, I could see his eyes were bloodshot. He looked drawn and pale.

He shrugged, falling into step beside me. "Just on

my way to Kara's."

"I thought you'd all be away by now - on your trip."

He shook his head. "Zoe's Dad left for the rigs early, so we need to wait till Roo's friends pick her up." Patrick kicked the ground, looking forlorn.

"Is everything okay?" I asked.

He hesitated, then made a face. "Of course. I just get these weird allergies to the plants around here sometimes." There was an awkward silence. We both knew it was the lamest excuse ever.

The silence became so uncomfortable I nearly blurted out that I had been to visit Christian. I was dying to talk to someone about it. In my head I kept replaying the conversation.

Patrick's pace slowed and he turned to me; all traces of arrogance gone from his demeanour.

"What's it like, your parents not being together anymore?"

I was taken aback by his direct question. I looked up at him and he held my gaze. A surge of sympathy flooded me as I recognised the fear.

"Are your parents still arguing?"

He nodded. "It's been constant lately. I think they actually hate each other."

I sighed. "Honestly, it's hard not having Dad here, having to start a new life. But I think the worst part for me was actually when it first started to unravel. The feeling that my life had been shaken upside down." I shivered at the memory of the first day dad moved out, during the 'temporary' break.

He smiled ruefully. "They're already not around much, which I guess is good because I can't take much more of listening to their fights. We all used to have so much fun together, you know? My sister and brothers don't really understand what's happening because they don't live at home anymore. It just used to be so different…" His voice trailed off.

I patted his arm awkwardly. "It'll be okay. Really."

He nodded and shot me an appreciative smile. We walked the rest of the way to Kara's in companionable silence.

As we approached my flat complex, Kara's bedroom window swung wide open. It took me a minute to register that she was perched on the sill, a spiral of smoke winding into the air. Patrick's demeanour instantly changed when he saw her. His self-assured swagger and cheeky grin returned as she poked her head out all the way to meet him in a kiss.

I waved awkwardly and she waved back.

"I missed you, sexy." Patrick grabbed her round the waist.

I looked past Kara and saw Zoe was inside, lying face down on Kara's bed, kicking her feet as she flicked through a magazine.

"Trip got delayed then?" I said.

"Yeah, we're not leaving till Wednesday now." Kara stubbed her cigarette out on the sill. "We're going to get a taxi pick-up here at eight a.m. and head into town for the train. Still plenty of space if you change your mind."

"Yeah, stop being a loser and just come," Zoe shouted, not bothering to turn round.

"You should." Patrick shot me a sincere smile and I almost warmed to the idea. I watched as he launched himself through the open window, laughing manically as he fell against Zoe, who whacked him over the head with her magazine.

I hesitated. "Thanks, but I've got plans for the rest

of the week."

Kara looked at me curiously. "Where were you today?"

"Just went into town with Daniel," I said casually.

Kara raised her eyebrows with a smile. "Oh, yeah."

"We're just friends," I said, gritting my teeth. "Anyway, I better go. Enjoy your trip."

"We will," she said breezily, muffling Zoe and Patrick's goodbye as she slammed the window shut.

As I walked up the steps to my flat, I wondered what a trip away with them would be like. A part of me longed to belong to their little group, although I was still wary. And too awkward – I would always be too much of a geek to really be accepted by them.

My thoughts returned to Christian as I unlocked the front door. His face was now clearly imprinted in my head; those eyes, such an intense blue. There was something mesmerising about him. The message from this Edgar bothered me though; someone knew I was trying to dig for the truth and didn't like it. I thought back to Daniel's story about Patrick burning his arm and the way he had warned me off when he found me in his bedroom. It seemed his style. But then today, Patrick seemed totally harmless, like his aggression and arrogance was all bravado.

As I swung the door open, I gaped in horror as I was confronted with the image of Mum sprawled across our sofa, half naked; a red velvety drape doing little to conceal her pale flesh. She was holding a glass of wine in one hand, giggling like a self-conscious girl. I was vaguely aware of Mr Harris sitting across from her. I did not want to look any more closely at him. It took my shocked senses a few more minutes to register the soft music and dim lighting.

I ran past them, hurling myself into my room, slamming the door shut behind me, hands shaking.

I could hear Mum's shrieks echoing down the hall. I'd never heard Mum use the 'F' word before. Until now. I squeezed my eyes shut, trying to block out the image of her on the sofa.

When I heard her steps thumping down the hall I jumped up. I threw my weight against the door, stopping her from opening it.

"Don't come in here!" I shouted. "I don't want to see you."

"I've got my dressing gown on," Mum breathed through the crack. "I'm so so sorry, Darcy. I'm bloody mortified. I thought you were going to be out all evening."

My hands were shaking as I pressed harder against the door. "Is this what you do when I'm not around? *Have...sex...with him...on our sofa?*" The last words squeaked out.

Silence. One heartbeat, two, three, four...

"What did you say?" I could picture Mum's lips pressed right up against the door. "Oh my god." Laughter. Proper snorting laughter through her nose.

A flare of anger sparked. "This isn't funny, Mum. This is disgusting. I can't believe you'd do this. Imagine if I'd walked in while you were in the middle of it with..." *Mr Harris.* Ew. I threw myself down on the bed, pulling a pillow over my head.

"Darcy," I heard Mum push the door open, was aware of her walking towards me. I pulled the pillow tighter over my head.

"Timothy...I mean, Mr Harris..."

"Call him Timothy. You calling him Mr Harris makes this one hundred times creepier."

"Okay, Timothy…" I felt her sit down on the bed. I curled my legs into a foetal position so she couldn't touch me. "We weren't up to anything…naughty." I shuddered at her using that word. "He was drawing me. Like life drawing, you know."

I pulled the pillow off my face. "Whatever, Mum. Just ask him to leave, please. I'm too embarrassed to see him. How am I supposed to face him at school after this?"

"He's more embarrassed than you, trust me." Mum tried to lean forward to stroke my cheek, but I moved my head. "Anyway, he's not naked, it was just me."

"Well, thank the lord for that," I said.

"Darcy, don't be angry…"

I refused to look at her.

"Did you have a nice trip to visit Daniel's cousin?"

"It was fine," I said.

"Okay, well give me a minute to tidy up the living room and then we can have dinner and you can tell me all about it."

As soon as Mum left, I jumped off the bed and pulled a backpack out of my wardrobe, a plan formulating in my mind. I could hear Mr Harris murmuring something to Mum as he exited, sounding apologetic.

I pulled my phone out of my bag and looked up Zoe's number, sending her a message before I changed my mind.

Hey, change of plan. I want to come on the trip after all. See you Wednesday morning.

My phoned buzzed in response almost instantly.

Good choice! Get ready for fun times.

The Trial

How has it come to this? Those were his mum's last words to him before his trial started. That's what Christian wanted to stand up and scream right now into the faces of each and every law official who sat in the room. Law officials had done nothing to silence the abuse he and his mum encountered on the run up to the trial. No one had helped them clear up the 'murderer' graffiti sprayed on their garage, or stopped the image being shared hundreds of times online. It terrified him, the feeling he'd already lost.

Everyone 'important' in the room today seemed bored. The judge had a far-away look in his eye, as if he were mentally ticking off his shopping list. But really, wasn't that what Christian was to him, just another item on his To Do list?

And his advocate? He was measured and calm and seemed to be saying all the right things, but there was no passion in his voice, no persuasion – just a series of complicated terms and black and white 'facts', none of which appeared to be having any impact whatsoever on the jury. Ted, his solicitor, bowed his head every time the advocate spoke, as if he had lost faith in their argument.

Then there was the jury. Christian felt sick every time he studied the row of people whose names had been chosen from a hat for his trial, like he was a prize in a raffle that no one wanted. Or maybe they did. At least one middle-aged woman and one studious-looking man in his thirties had an air of excitement, studying Christian intently and scribbling notes in their pads. He bet anything that they would have read the online feeds about him, possibly contributed to them, even if they denied any knowledge. A judge would never really know what information they had consumed before today. How could it be an unbiased trial? His name had spread online like a contagious disease. It felt like his trial had been half played out already before anyone had even reached a courtroom.

Christian scanned across the row. A couple of men who looked like they had rolled out of a pub. One didn't look quite right – he had sat with his mouth open most of the morning, vacant eyes staring at his pen. A younger woman – hair scraped back, eyebrows painted on too heavily – spent most of the first hour yawning and fidgeting with her bracelet. He noticed that her talon nails sparkled pink and silver every time she moved her hands.

An older woman frowned at him quite a bit, her head shaking from side to side whenever the prosecution put across their argument against him.

Christian wanted to shake the judge and demand a re-selection. How was it possible that a group of imbeciles got to decide the fate of his life? As he listened to the monotonous tones of his advocate, he had to fight the urge to stand up and call a halt to it all.

I can tell you what you need to hear. The words kept running around his head in a loop, booming louder as his eyes fell upon his mum.

She sat with head bowed, half leaning against Mr Harris. Mr Harris met his gaze, eyes grave and steady. Christian didn't look away.

Tell them. He could almost sense Mr Harris's words as if they were floating out of his mind and across the court room towards him.

Tell them the truth and let's all go home.

Chapter Eighteen

As soon as my phone alarm vibrated under my pillow I shot out of bed, quietly turning on the bedside lamp. Six thirty. Way too early to be up and about on a holiday, my tired brain grumbled as I felt around for my jeans and top.

I had co-operated the past two evenings - having dinner with Mum, trying to act like everything was completely normal between us, even although my whole body felt like it had been shaken upside down any time I looked at the sofa. It wasn't like I was a prude, or oblivious to the fact that Mum was a woman, Mr Harris was a man, clearly…but it just didn't seem right. Even if they were dressing it up as art. Mum didn't seem to get how it would make me feel. But how *did* it make me feel? I didn't fully understand this anger that was simmering inside. Shouldn't I be happy for them?

I went to the loo and didn't bother to flush, not wanting to wake Mum before her alarm. She wouldn't be getting up for work for another hour. She usually crept around to give me a lie-in during the holidays, so as long as I kept my bedroom door shut, she probably wouldn't clock I wasn't here.

But just in case, I scribbled a note and left it on my empty bed:

Headed to Fee's early.

Good old Fee. It had taken a lot of text grovelling to persuade her to cover, especially as we had barely messaged for weeks. Eventually I lied and told her I was sneaking off with a new boyfriend to lose my big V and promised to give her all of the details on my return. That soon shocked her into submission. She did me proud, surviving a half-hour interrogation call from Mum, who demanded to know everything she'd been up to the past few months, then what us girls had planned during my visit.

As I grabbed my bag and phone, I debated messaging Daniel. Something stopped me. Maybe part of me was scared he'd want to come along too. I didn't want anyone there trying to tell me what to do - stopping me having fun.

A click of the letterbox alerted me to mail. I saw the handwriting as I approached, feeling a jolt of excitement and fear. *Thank god it had arrived before I left.* I tore the envelope open, realising Christian must have written this soon after our visit, for it to arrive so quickly.

Dear Darcy,

Thanks for coming to visit. It was good to meet you. You seemed a lot quieter in real life than in your letters. I guess this place has that ability – to suck the life right out of you as soon as you walk through the doors, what with its depressing aura. I'm sorry if that idiot upset you at the end. Most of the guys in here aren't very bright and tend to use aggressive forms of communication. It sometimes feels like I'm living in a different world here, like in cave men times, except we don't have food to hunt, just each other.

I was a prime target when I first arrived. But they've backed off a bit since I started to draw comic strips of our life in here. I get to write the script any way I want, so I make the most violent of my inmates the heroes in a lot of the 'adventures' and the guards are all stupid, with buck teeth. They like that – my fellow inmates, I mean. I think it gives them a sense of power. It gives me a sense of power too, of control. I get to write my own ending every day, like a magical choose-your-own-adventure story.

I'm just telling you this because I could sense your worry. Thanks for worrying. But I am OK. Please tell Daniel too that I am OK.

I hope you come back to visit again sometime soon. Maybe alone next time? Because I don't know you so well, I think it would be easier having you visit me. I always feel this sense of doom and guilt whenever I see Daniel or Mum because I know they're also feeling a hopeless sense of doom and guilt. Such is this life.

Alright, Darcy. Take it easy.

Later,

Christian Henderson

I smiled, relieved that even although he'd thought I was quiet, he still wanted me to visit again. I re-read it one last time then hurried to my room, tucking it inside the jewellery box along with the other letters.

*

Kara was waiting at her open door when I reached the bottom of the stairs. She motioned me in, whispering that her gran was still asleep, so we had to be quiet. Her hair was hanging damp around her shoulders, her face pale and make-up free, as if she had just come out a shower. She looked younger and less intimidating without her make-up, but still beautiful.

We slipped into her bedroom and she shut the door. I nervously sat down on the bed, careful not to disrupt the pile of clothes strewn across it. Kara sat at her dressing table quickly blow-drying her hair – I marvelled at the way it fell into perfect waves without her appearing to do much. I smoothed at my hair self-consciously, wondering if her perfection was genetics or a learned skill.

"So, what made you change your mind?" Kara asked, running black liner under one eye.

I hesitated, the image of Mum on the sofa flashing in my head. My cheeks burned at the thought of telling Kara; she would never let me hear the end of it if I mentioned it. I shrugged. "I thought it might be fun."

"I have to say I was surprised. You always look a bit nervous around us."

My blush deepened. "Do I?"

Kara leaned in closer towards the mirror as she applied mascara, her mouth opening into an 'o' of concentration. "*Do* we make you nervous?"

I was taken aback by her directness and was a bit unsure how to answer. "I guess I can be awkward around new people."

"Well, I'm sure after this trip you'll get to know us a whole lot better."

The statement didn't exactly sound like a reassurance. I gripped at my bag, wondering if I was making a mistake. But I needed to get away for a bit - to extract the memory of my half-naked mother from my head. And getting to know Kara and the others better would surely encourage them to trust me, maybe open up a bit more.

Kara fluffed at her hair, casting her reflection an approving look. Her eyes met mine in the mirror and I quickly averted my gaze.

She turned to look at me directly. "If you get to know me you might be surprised."

"What do you mean?"

Kara shrugged. "I think people think I'm a cold bitch. I guess I am a lot of the time. But it's the way I've had to be. Tough, I mean. It's how I've learned to put up with my mum's crap over the years. She's never liked me much."

"I'm sure that's not true…" I started to protest.

Kara shot me a patronising look. "What would you know? Your mum seems pretty cool."

"Most of the time." *When she wasn't posing half-naked for my art teacher,* I was tempted to add.

"My gran is so decent. God knows how her daughter turned out to be such a car crash. But it's not the same, you know. I've barely seen my parents the past year." Kara laid down her brush.

I felt a pang when I realised it was going to be another two months now before I saw Dad, thanks to me declining his offer to stay with him this holiday. I shot Kara a sympathetic smile.

She shook her head, like she hadn't meant to get so personal. "Anyway, this trip is going to be fun, right?"

She grabbed at the clothes on the bed, packing them into a cute little suitcase that sat on the floor. As I watched her insert what appeared to be two weeks' outfits, I resisted asking if she was staying on at the cabin longer than a few days. She shoved her make-up bag on top, hesitating.

"Let me touch up your make-up for you."

Before I could protest, she was sitting next to me, ordering me to shut my eyes as she buffed at my face with powders, dabbed on eyeshadow and gently lined the top of my eyelids.

"Open," she commanded, and I opened my eyes, looking at her uncertainly.

She grinned, handing me a metal contraption. "Now you *do* look nervous. These curl your eyelashes."

She grabbed them back off me. "Like this," she demonstrated.

I gingerly did the same.

"Here's some mascara." She handed me a brand that was a bit more sophisticated than the cheap one I sometimes wore when I could be bothered, which wasn't very often.

"Perfect. You've got such a cute little face. You should show it off more often. Look." Kara opened a hand mirror and I took it from her, marvelling at how startling and blue my eyes now looked. I touched my skin. And she had magically rubbed out the sprinkle of spots across my t-zone. Even my freckles were less pronounced. If only I'd worn make-up like this when I'd gone to see Christian. I quickly dismissed the thought.

"Thanks." I smiled, handing back the mirror. "Are we still getting a taxi to the station?"

Kara checked her phone. "Yeah. Patrick slept in, but he's just called the taxi and will pick up Zoe on the way here. Let's go."

I glanced at my reflection in her dresser mirror and held my head higher. This *was* going to be fun. *I* was going to be fun. And maybe, just maybe I would get a bit closer to the truth.

*

For the first hour of the train journey, Zoe slept and Kara kept nuzzling Patrick's neck. It made conversation with them a bit awkward, so I flicked open an iBook on my phone, hoping this wasn't going to be a pattern for the whole trip. Maybe I should have asked Daniel to come along after all.

"You should make the most of phone time just now, Darcy. We rarely get reception up at the cabin," Patrick said.

"I'm just reading a book I downloaded," I said, realising I should text Mum as a back up to the note. If she tried to call me later and my phone was dead, she'd panic. I quickly typed out a message:

Hi Mum, Hope you got my note okay. Fee had plans for us to go to see a lunchtime film at the GFT, so wanted to call by hers first for brunch and drop my stuff. Have a good day. Love D x

It worried me slightly how easy I was finding it to lie to her. It had always been a rule between us – openness and honesty. Maybe she would have been fine about me going to the cabin. Happy, even, that I was making new friends. That's what she wanted me to do.

"You're just like Zoe, always got her nose stuck in some book." Kara rolled her eyes.

"Hmm?" Zoe stirred at the mention of her name. She yawned, glancing out the window. "How long have I been napping?"

"Too long." Patrick nudged her foot with his trainer. "Let's crack open the champers."

"We're saving it for later in the hot tub." Kara slapped his hand as he started to unzip his bag.

A grin spread across Patrick's face. "Lucky me. I get to share a hot tub with three pretty ladies this trip." He winked and a cold sweat swept across me.

Hot tub? No one had mentioned this to me.

"Keep dreaming, Patrick," Zoe murmured.

"I didn't bring a swimming costume," I said.

Patrick raised an eyebrow. "Even better."

Kara punched him on the arm. "Don't be vulgar."

"Sorry, sweetpea." He hooked his arm around Kara's neck, pulling her towards him, kissing her loudly on the cheek.

Zoe turned to me. "You can borrow mine. I'm not really a fan of the water."

It wasn't the water that bothered me. The thought of revealing my skinny pale legs to this group filled me with dread. Patrick's eyes locked with mine and he shot me a flirtatious smile. There was no trace of the vulnerability I'd seen the other evening.

I wondered if I had actually dreamt seeing him cry. I turned my attention back to reading, absorbing none of the words as my mind flickered over various doubts about this trip.

A message popped up from Daniel.

Hey, what you up to today? Want to come over and play pool?

Regret stabbed at me. The thought of playing pool with Daniel was so appealing. *But it was safe. Boring.*

Hey, I'm on my way to visit an old school friend, sorry. Catch up with you at the weekend.

I wanted my story to match with the one I'd told Mum, in case she tried to contact him.

Ok. Catch you another time.

"Is that Daniel you're messaging?" Zoe asked, glancing at my phone out of the corner of her eye.

"Um, yeah," I said.

"Why didn't you ask him along?" Kara asked.

I shrugged. "I didn't think he'd want to come."

"He doesn't like us much, eh?" Patrick said.

Thinking back to the story Daniel had told me about Patrick burning his arm and slashing the tyres of his BMX, I wanted to say, *Can you blame him?*

"What's his theory about what happened to Louise? Does he think I did it?" Patrick sat forward.

Kara's mouth set in a grim line. "Patrick..."

"Did you do it?"

There was a stunned silence. My heart thudded. *Did I really just ask that out loud?*

Patrick laughed and Kara put a warning hand on his arm. "Can we please just change the subject?"

"What do you think, Darcy?" he asked, eyes flashing.

"I'm not sure."

"So, you think there's a chance I could have? Interesting." He pretended to scratch his chin in concentration. "Very brave of you to come along to a remote cabin with a potential murderer."

Very stupid of you. The realisation hit the pit of my stomach. I gripped my phone tighter. What if it *had* been him? And what if he was Edgar?

"I loved Louise a lot. And I miss her," Patrick said, his voice softening. Kara looked like he had slapped her across the face. "We all loved her," he added, squeezing Kara's hand, like he was reassuring her that it wasn't a love like the one he had for her.

"Even although she could be an absolute bitch at times," Kara said.

Patrick frowned. "Not so bad that she deserved to be killed."

There was a charged silence. Kara didn't back up his sentiment. Zoe was gazing out the window, like she had chosen not to be part of the conversation.

"Christian Henderson was put away for a reason, Darcy," Patrick continued. "I know you've become best buds with Daniel, who I'm sure is feeding you all sorts of crap about how innocent and wronged Christian was during the trial, but it was a fair investigation. There can be no denying the fact that Christian was a bit of a strange un, and he was all over Louise that night."

"While you were all over Kara?" Zoe piped up.

Patrick ignored her and went on. "Louise could be a bit of a tease. She probably led the poor boy on a bit too much and he got mad when she retracted. I think she might have laughed at him. Can you imagine how humiliating that must have been for him?"

"You must have been a bit annoyed too, if he was flirting with your girlfriend?" I said.

Patrick shrugged. "Well, I was a bit pre-occupied that evening." He squeezed Kara's hand and she appeared to melt against him in response.

I thought back to the photograph of Patrick and Kara kissing at the party. Christian's story had been that Patrick had attacked him in a jealous rage, and that Louise had tried to intervene. That was the account that had been published on forums, to explain Louise's scratches on Christian's arm. But if Patrick had been truly pre-occupied with Kara that evening, *would* he have been that bothered?

"It's easy to trust the wrong people sometimes, Darcy," Patrick said. "Personally, I always respect the arseholes; at least their flaws are right there in your face. I bet you think Mr Harris is the best thing since sliced bread too."

The mention of Mr Harris sent a jolt through my body.

Kara shot Patrick a questioning look.

"He's another strange un. Paid way too much attention to Louise, inviting her to his exhibitions, encouraging her to join his after-school art clubs. I think he even asked to paint her portrait, privately, like at his house."

An overwhelming feeling of nausea washed over me, Patrick's voice becoming a distant echo, like I was having an out of body experience.

"And then he started dating Christian's mum. Acting like he was trying to protect them both, when it was obvious to me that he was just making sure he was as close to the investigation as possible to cover his own back - to make sure the police stayed on Christian's trail and off his."

"Don't be ridiculous, Patrick." Kara slapped him on the arm. She turned to me. "Don't listen to him, Darcy. I told you before, Louise was an attention seeker. And knew how to manipulate men. *Clearly.*" Kara rolled her eyes at Patrick.

The nausea was now hitting me in waves. I stood up, legs shaking. "I'm just going to the toilet," I murmured, half aware of Kara chiding Patrick as I walked away.

"Don't you know he's dating her mum now, *stupid.* That really upset her. Can we at least try to have a bit of fun today?"

The motion of the train made it hard to walk in a straight line. I grabbed on to headrests as I jolted from side to side, trying to steady myself. Christian had said in his letter that Mr Harris was one of the good ones - that he had supported his mum. But it had *got complicated*. What kind of complicated?

Trees scraped against the window glass as we sped through the countryside. Maybe I should get off at the next stop - go home, talk to Mum.

And say what? Tell her that her new boyfriend might have been involved in a teenage girl's murder?

PRIVATE MESSAGE to Darcy Thomas
From: Edgar

I know you've been writing to him. And arranged a visit. Christian is too polite to tell you to get lost. But I'm not. He doesn't think you'll figure it out. I think you're too goddamn nosy. Always full of so many questions. And you're already noticing too much.

I'm not sure you're taking me seriously. I want you to know I will do ANYTHING to stop the truth coming out and I notice things too. I am always watching every little thing you do.

Enjoy your visit to the cabin. I hope you're not afraid of the dark.

Chapter Nineteen

"Are you okay? We were wondering where you'd got to."

I jumped at the voice, my phone clattering to the ground, sliding along the carpet and under a chair.

"Sorry, let me help you..."

"No, it's fine. I've got it."

My back twisted painfully as I thrust my hand towards the phone, desperate to re-read the message, but at the same time wanting to delete it and throw my phone out the window – to take any threat of 'Edgar' away.

Zoe looked genuinely worried, stepping back to allow me to straighten up. "You don't look so good, Darcy. Is it because of what Patrick was saying, about Mr Harris?"

I shook my head, wanting to confront them all, to ask about 'Edgar'.

"Kara's right. Louise will have exaggerated any attention from Mr Harris to make Patrick jealous or to get some sympathy. She never cared how her lies affected people."

I nodded, sliding my phone back inside my jean pocket. I noticed with dismay that we were approaching the stop before our destination. Should I get off now, and head home? If 'Edgar' knew I was on my way to the cabin, clearly 'Edgar' was right here on the train with me. Only Zoe, Kara and Patrick knew where I was going.

"Want some chocolate?" Zoe held up a bar, a shy smile on her face. I knew she was thanking me again for the sympathy I had shown her at lunch the other day.

"Thanks." I took it, relaxing a little. I started to follow Zoe back to our seats.

"You know, I'm glad you decided to come along. I wasn't sure I could handle being alone with Patrick and Kara up there, they can get so mushy. And don't get mad…"

She hesitated and I stumbled, nearly colliding with her.

"I ran into Daniel outside my house this morning when he was out doing his paper round, and asked if he wanted to join us. He said he would think about it, maybe come up tomorrow."

"You what?" My face flamed at the outright lie I had told Daniel earlier. His invitation to play pool must have been a test to see if I would tell him.

"I'm guessing he didn't mention it when you were messaging? Did he change his mind?"

I sighed. "He will have now. I told him I was going to visit a friend."

"Oh," Zoe said. "Sorry. I didn't realise you didn't want him to know."

"It's fine. It was partly so he would back up my story to my Mum."

"She doesn't know you're here either?"

"No. She can be funny about that stuff – you know, letting me go off on remote trips with friends she's never met…"

Zoe looked wistful for a moment and I wondered if her mum would have been the same. Maybe her dad was so pre-occupied with his job that he didn't care so much where she went.

We arrived back at our seats to find Patrick and Kara snogging the faces off each other, drawing disapproving looks from the couple at the table beside ours.

Zoe cleared her throat loudly as she slid back into her seat. Kara broke away first, running a hand through her tousled hair. She looked up at me. "Everything okay?"

I nodded, avoiding Patrick's piercing gaze. "Fine. I just wanted some alone time."

"I hope you're not going to be an anti-social bore on this trip, Darcy." Patrick pinged his empty Coke can at me and I caught it deftly, whacking it back to hit him on the chest.

Zoe smirked. "You can talk. I hope the two of you plan to come up for air."

"There's enough Patrick to go around, little Zoe, if you're feeling left out." He grinned. Kara slapped him on the arm.

The mechanical voice on the train announced that we were approaching our stop. Patrick jumped up, pulling his jacket down from the overhead rack.

Kara unzipped her bag and slid off her heeled platforms, swapping them for boots.

"It's a bit of a trek to the cabin," Zoe explained, seeing me clock Kara's change of shoes. "We'll get a bus some of the way, but then we've got to walk through a lot of countryside."

"Glad I wore my trainers then." I forced a smile, trying to ignore the panicked voice in my head, telling me that I was crazy to even consider going anywhere remote with this group.

As we stepped onto the platform, a band of dark clouds drifted across the sky, casting a strange half-light over the quaint Highland town. I breathed in the cold air, my head clearing after the train's stuffiness. Even in this muted light, the scenery was breathtaking, hills dominating the landscape.

A gravel path led us out of the station, towards the town centre and to the bus stop. A group of hikers joined us, studying maps and drinking from flasks. As I watched one of them peel a banana, I realised I hadn't packed any snacks.

"Is there a shop near the cabin?" I asked.

Patrick gestured towards the row of shops across from the bus stop. "This is it." He tapped the bottom of his backpack. "Don't worry, Darcy. I've brought plenty of supplies – cheesy pasta, crisps, biscuits, booze…"

"I've got the veggies and bread," Zoe said.

"Maybe I should get some stuff…" I started to say, just as a green and white bus rumbled towards us.

"It's fine, Darcy," Kara said breezily. "There's always loads of supplies in the cabin freezer. Like pizza."

Patrick paid our bus fares, motioning for us to go on ahead and find a seat up the back. As we walked up the aisle, faces stared as if we had flashing lights above our heads announcing we were from out of town. Two old ladies in matching anoraks and purple rinses smiled as I slid into the seat behind them.

"Would you like a mint, dear?" One of them turned to me, hands shaking as she held out a stripy sweet. "Humbugs."

"Thank you." I took the sweets, trying not to stare at her pantomime make-up: white powder settling into the lines on her face, tangerine lipstick bleeding at the corners of her mouth.

I turned to hand Zoe one, but her head was stuck in a book, giving the impression she had transported herself to another land. Judging by the ghoulish face on the cover, and blood-dripping title, it was no land I wanted to visit.

I looked down at her bag, the zips not quite shut. I noticed another couple of books, and what looked like a couple of letters. It made me think back to Christian's letter, asking me to go back to visit him alone. I would like that. I wanted to quiz him more about why Mr Harris had ended it with Christian's mum. I could also quiz him about Edgar; he must have read his postings too and would maybe have some ideas about his identity.

We travelled the rest of the journey in silence, the clouds darkening more the further the bus drove into the countryside. I zipped my jacket up tighter, hoping the charcoal sky wasn't an omen.

As soon as we descended from the bus, the rain started. The wind raged, so that no matter how tight I pulled my hood around my head, my face got a pelting.

"We have to go down this hill to get onto the right path," Patrick shouted, motioning me to follow him.

I tried to keep up, the field sucking at my cheap canvas trainers, my socks already soaked through. I wished I'd invested in some proper walking boots. The thought of drying off beside an open fire in the cabin kept me going.

As I half slid, half walked down the first dip of the hill, the rain suddenly stopped, like someone had turned off a tap. The clouds parted enough to allow a flash of sun. I smiled, pushing my hood back.

"Thank god for that," Kara huffed. "Remind me again why we decided to come here. Next time we go to my parents' Villa in France."

I unzipped my jacket, trying to shake off some of the rain. It had soaked through the top of my jeans. I reached into my pocket to rescue my phone. My heart jumped when I noticed five missed calls from Mum. *Crap.* Wasn't a note and a text enough for her?

Just as I was debating returning the calls, the phone vibrated in my hand, *Mum* dancing across the screen.

"If you want to talk to anyone, now would be the time to do it," Patrick said. "We're about to hit a dead zone."

I hesitated, then hit answer. Before I even had a chance to say hello, Mum's voice was ranting in my ear.

"Darcy, you need to come home right NOW young lady…"

I blinked. How the hell had she seen through my lie so quickly? No wonder I found it so hard to rebel when I had a mind reader for a mother…

"I found the letters. The letters from that boy, that murderer." Her voice went up five octaves as she said 'murderer'.

I kept walking, a dread washing over me.

"I was looking for those earrings you borrowed and saw a letter sticking out of your jewellery box. When I saw the stamp on it I wondered what on earth was going on, why on earth would you be receiving a letter from anyone connected with the prison service… then I found the others…"

"You went through my stuff?" I interjected. "That's such an invasion of privacy, Mum."

"Do not start me, young lady. Do not start," Mum growled, sounding mildly hysterical. *"What are you playing at, Darcy? You promised that you would stop with this obsession, that you would stop reading about this Christian Henderson. But instead you start writing to him? Writing to a boy who stabbed a young girl? This is serious. This is murder we're talking*

about. A violent boy who could..."

Mum's voice faded mid-sentence, the line going dead.

I stopped walking, staring helplessly at the screen.

Patrick shot me a rueful smile. "Told ya. That's us hit the dead zone I'm afraid."

As I watched the three of them disappear further into the woods, Mum's panicked voice stayed with me.

What are you playing at, Darcy. This is murder.

And now here I was, walking into a 'dead zone' with three 'friends' I barely knew.

The Trial: Part 2

"Just be honest, it's not looking good, is it?"

Christian's solicitor, Ted, was increasingly avoiding eye contact as the trial progressed. He shuffled papers and squeezed his empty coffee cup, the polystyrene popping in the silence. He cast glances at the door and Christian knew he was willing his advocate to return to answer this question.

Christian's Mum sat forward in her chair, eyes not leaving Ted's face for a second. Christian realised she hadn't blinked once, as if caught in a staring contest, just daring his solicitor to reply with the wrong answer.

"I don't want to lie to you…" Ted scratched his mop of hair. He had patches of uneven stubble on each cheek; this irritated Christian. Ted could at least present a together, smart front to fool the jury into thinking his team was totally on top of things – to give them the impression that they were confident during declarations of Christian's innocence.

Ted shuffled more papers. "The prosecution came up with some strong arguments earlier. Mostly circumstantial, obviously, with the speculation that you had an obsession with Louise. But the sketches are a good back-up for that speculation. And those witnesses, those girls from the party saying it was you who followed Louise upstairs, even though I know you say she came to find you. And their stories sounded plausible – that they heard shouting coming from the bedroom and saw you running down the stairs with blood on you…"

"Those girls don't even go to my school," Christian interrupted. "I bet they weren't even at the party. It was like they were reading straight from a script off those f'ing forum postings."

"Christian." His mum shot him a look, like swearing was worse than this. Worse than being accused of losing it and stabbing a girl at a party because of some jealous lustful obsession.

"And, of course, your DNA on Louise, your skin under her nails, and your fingerprints on the knife. That's the clear evidence. The fact that only *your* fingerprints were found and it was your knife."

"Everyone at that party was in costume. Patrick was wearing surgical gloves. Tell the advocate, Gregor, to push that line more."

A flicker of irritation crossed Ted's face. Christian read the expression, *Don't tell us how to do our jobs, boy. You are the client, we are the professionals.* "If we keep pushing the costume line, Christian, it just reminds the jury that you put yours in the wash as soon as you reached home that night."

"I want you to put me on the stand," Christian said.

Ted shook his head.

"I am begging you to let me fight my case. Half of this is made-up speculation. It's all twisting stories, creating a distorted picture of me. I want them to hear my real story."

"You don't understand, Christian. These prosecution lawyers are highly skilled. They know how to break you down. Give them ten minutes with you up there and I guarantee they will have *you* believing you did it."

Christian sat back in his chair, clenching his fist. His mum tried to lay a reassuring hand on his. He pulled away.

"That's the problem, isn't it?" Christian said. "You think I'm guilty, don't you?"

Ted shook his head. "I think you need to take five to calm down, Christian. Going back in there demonstrating any signs of aggression is not a good plan."

Ted exited the room, away to chat with the advocate. Christian turned to his mum, trying to ignore the tears glistening in her eyes.

"Mum, they don't have enough on me. This is ridiculous. Those girls were making stuff up. Lies they've been reading online."

Christian thought back to the conversations he'd had with the only other person who really knew the truth. He had been so certain that even if he were to go on trial there would be nothing to worry about. There wasn't enough evidence. The fact that no one had picked up on all of their actions that night was proof.

I promise I won't let you down. Christian remembered saying those words with such conviction. He still had an out. He had only ever promised to keep going with the trial if it looked like nothing would come of it. But now every part of his shaking body told him it was getting serious. Really serious. And there were still parts he felt he didn't know. Parts of that night that were still unclear when he thought back, trying to piece everything together. He drummed his fingers on the table, not even knowing what he could say. Anything that came out of his mouth now would sound like proper lies. Words that would damage.

He checked the clock. The next few hours would define what kind of person he really was.

Christian thought back to the night his dad left. A noise had disturbed him and he had stumbled halfway down the stairs, staring in sleepy confusion at the dark figure exiting the front door, bag slung over his shoulder. At first Christian had been alarmed, thinking they were being burgled.

Then the figure had turned around, a sheepish smile etched across his face.

"I'm sorry, son. I have to go."

No goodbye. No explanation. Just, 'I have to go' as a half-arsed apology. Sneaking off in the middle of the night, like a coward, abandoning him.

There was no worse feeling than someone walking out on you, leaving you when things got too hard. Leaving you feeling alone and scared.

His thoughts skipped to months earlier, after the initial police interviews.

"What if they find out? I can't get put away…I just can't…"

Christian tried to offer reassurance whenever they met to unpick the questions asked. He was certain there was no way the police would have enough evidence. It would remain a secret, between them. He wasn't going to talk.

He recognised the haunted expression, the desperate fear when the life you thought was so safe and so certain was ripped away from you one night. One night you would never forget.

Christian watched the clock hand *tick, tick, tick*, creeping past the numbers. *Five, six, seven, eight, we're in court to decide your fate.*

The verdict was ready to be delivered. As Christian walked down the corridor he had grown to hate, he half wondered if they would be there, sitting in the side lines, listening, waiting to hear. When the doors opened and he stepped inside the court room, he didn't even look around to check.

Instead his focus was on the jury and when he saw a smile twitch on the old lady's face, he knew.

Guilty.

That word sounded like hate, disgust and spite all rolled in to one.

Chapter Twenty

The queen bed dominated the attic room, the patchwork blanket a homely offset to what looked like a silk duvet set underneath. The lamp in the corner cast an orange glow across the wooden beams in the ceiling, the mahogany wardrobe and accompanying furniture adding to the warmth. Patrick and Kara insisted I sleep up in the attic to give me some privacy. Zoe had already started to unpack her bag up there. After some discussion, she reluctantly agreed to sleep in a room downstairs, but I could tell that she was a bit put out. I hoped it wouldn't place a damper on the evening's mood.

I launched myself at the bed, mattress springs squeaking in protest. I sighed happily as my head sank into the fortress of pillows. I wiggled my toes inside my slippers; so dry and warm. Such a welcome contrast to earlier.

I rubbed at my calves, thinking back to the miles of fields we must have covered in the afternoon, when the weather brightened. It felt good escaping to open spaces, away from everything at home. I eyed my muddy trainers in the corner of the room, wondering if they would survive many more marshy walks.

Patrick's voice echoed up the wooden staircase. "Dinner's in five."

"Okay." I shouted back, reaching across the bed to plug in my phone. I willed the bars to rise, hopeful I would get reception at some point. A pang of guilt hit me when I thought about how mad Mum would be, thinking I had cut her off mid-call. I also knew she'd be worried if she was trying to reach me and kept getting directed to my voicemail. Poor Fee. She was sure to get the brunt of Mum's rage. There was no way she would sustain my lie now.

If there was no option but to take the flack when I returned, I owed it to myself to make the most of this trip.

I rifled through my backpack, tempted to change into my pyjamas or even just remain in the white fluffy robe from the bathroom. Kara had directed me to a whole cupboard full of them, like a stolen collection from hotels. I decided on jeans and woolly jumper. Keep with the country theme.

As I pulled the jumper over my head, I paused, hearing a loud tap, tap, tapping. I stood still, straining to hear it again. Nothing. Just the wind howling against the window. I pulled on my jeans.

TAP TAP TAP. I spun around, tiptoeing over to the wall. I hesitated, then touched my cheek against the cool brick. Tap, tap, tap, tap, tap. I held my breath. It sounded like someone knocking from outside.

"Hello?" I called out. "Is that one of you messing about?" I pressed my ear closer. I could hear something faint, like a humming…a moan?

I jumped back. "Stop messing about. This isn't funny." I ran to the door and yanked it open. I paused, hearing Zoe and Kara laughing downstairs, too far away to be playing tricks on me. Patrick…? I could smell pizza cooking in the kitchen, then heard him shout through to the girls, asking what they wanted to drink.

I turned back to look inside the room. The window rattled as the wind rose in waves. I plucked up the courage to pull back the curtain…to find a loose branch knocking against the pane. I decided the acoustics of the room must be making the rattle echo through the walls. That, and my overactive imagination. *Keep it together, Darcy.*

The idea of being with the others suddenly seemed very appealing. I hurried down the creaky staircase, chewing my nails and realising I'd taken off my rings before my bath. As I strode along the hallway to the bathroom, steam and the aroma of my lavender oil curled out from behind the door, calming me.

I spotted the rings by the sink. As I slid them onto my fingers, my attention was drawn to the mirror. Letters had started to form in the steam:

Please help me.

I jumped back, instinctively turning to check behind me.

"Darcy, what's taking you so long?" Kara's voice echoed along the hallway.

I stared back at the mirror. It had to be Patrick messing about, trying to scare us. I wiped away the letters and followed the smell of pizza.

Zoe and Kara were in the lounge, on the sofa nearest the fire, feet resting on the edge of the massive oak table, sipping drinks from what looked like silver goblets. Their heads were practically touching as they whispered conspiringly. My eyes were drawn to a board, at the centre of the table, adorned with elaborate calligraphy. As I moved closer I could make out *Yes* and *No* in the two top corners, and the alphabet across the middle...*A, B, C*... I scanned across a series of numbers. Then... *Goodbye*.

The fire crackled.

"Pizza?"

I jumped as Patrick thrust a plate under my nose. I took it from him, still studying the Ouija board.

Kara turned, alerted to my presence. "There she is." Her voice was flat, like she was bored. "We thought you'd drowned in the bath."

I shook my head, meaning to speak, but my tongue felt heavy. I could feel something like fear creeping up my throat as Zoe and Patrick stared at me, then smirked at each other when they saw me eyeing the board.

"I'm guessing you've never used one of these before?" Zoe tapped at *Goodbye* with her toe. Her toenails were painted black and I wanted to make a reassuring joke in my head that this was like a weird Halloween party gone wrong. But then I remembered: Louise had been at a Halloween party when she'd said…goodbye. *It's too early for Halloween*, I told myself.

I stuffed the slice of pizza into my mouth, cheese sticking to my teeth and pepperoni burning off half my skin. I welcomed the distraction. I chewed quickly, trying not to think about the creepy stories my old friends used to share about Ouija boards: of windows smashing, children falling down stairs, a finger falling off…that one a particularly ridiculous story Fee had taken great delight in telling during a midnight feast when we were about ten. It was always stories about a 'cousin' or 'family friend'. We had all been too chicken to actually experience the board first hand.

Kara smiled as she twirled the 'pointer' round in one hand, gripping her goblet in the other.

"Drink up, drink up." Patrick handed me one of the silver goblets and I sniffed. Sickly sweet, laced with something sharp.

"What is it?" I peered into the pool of darkness.

"Buckle-up Bubblegum. My very own fabulous

creation." Patrick winked and threw his head back, glugging his down like lemonade.

I took a sip, nearly gagging on the sugar overload.

Zoe and Kara had stopped talking, the hiss and crackle of the fire accentuated in the silence. I drank faster, trying to distract myself from the unease creeping up my legs.

Floorboards creaked above us. I looked up. "Is someone else here?"

"Why don't we find out?" Kara clicked the pointer against the Ouija board and Zoe giggled.

I shot her a wry smile. "Very funny. It's just earlier, when I was upstairs, I could hear tapping… And who was the joker who wrote in the mirror?"

Zoe took the pointer from Kara and slid it around the board. *"You came tapping, tapping, at my chamber door… darkness there and nothing more."*

I strained to hear Zoe's whispers as Patrick pulled me towards him in a head lock. "It's alright, little Darcy. We'll protect you. It's just a creaky old cabin and the wind is howling up a storm out there tonight."

I wriggled free of his grasp, rubbing at my neck. I was uncomfortably aware of Kara shooting me jealous glances and I moved to sit on the woollen rug, distancing myself from Patrick.

"So how does this magic talking board work exactly?" Patrick asked, biting on the end of a large slice of pizza, making the cheese stretch from between his teeth.

Kara tucked her hair behind her ears, sitting forward, leaning over the board. "We need to ask it a question."

"Okay, I've got one." Patrick swallowed a mouthful. "What colour is Darcy's underwear?"

I glared up at him.

"Don't be lame, Patrick." Zoe rolled her eyes.

Kara's expression darkened. "Why don't you ask a question, Darcy? You're never usually short of those. What would you like to know?"

A part of Edgar's message flashed through my head: *Always full of so many questions.*

Kara positioned the pointer under the letters, Zoe's finger touching the edge.

"You have to put your finger on the pointer too," Zoe told me.

I hesitated, stretching out my hand, hoping none of them noticed the tremble. I wasn't brave enough to ask the questions circling my head.

"Was Louise really murdered that night at the party?" Kara's voice was clear and confident.

The three of us stared at the pointer. I could feel my pulse throbbing in the tip of my finger. The fire cracked and I jumped. Patrick chuckled.

"Shut up, Patrick," Kara said. "It won't work if you start joking about."

My finger twitched and the pointer started to slide up the board.

Zoe shrieked and I let go, watching in horror as the pointer slid towards the *Yes* in the top left-hand corner.

"Stop messing about, Kara." Zoe's eyes widened in fear as the pointer stopped on the word.

Kara shook her head, lips trembling. "I'm not doing anything, I swear."

I looked up at Patrick, who had abandoned his pizza. He frowned. "Very funny, ladies."

"Who was it?" Kara's voice shook and I wanted to tell her to stop, but also wanted to see what would happen next.

Kara and Zoe gaped at each other in fearful

anticipation. No movement.

Patrick sat forward, his leg brushing against my shoulder blades. "Tell us who it was. Who murdered Louise?"

Kara whimpered as the pointer began to slide back down the board, scraping across the letters towards the Y….

O…U pause K…N…O…W

"You know," I whispered.

A bang from down the hall made us all jump; Zoe screamed.

Patrick held up a hand. "It's okay. I left the study window open earlier. It'll just be the door blowing shut."

"Well go and check, will you," Kara said.

Patrick stood up, puffing out his chest. "Anyone care to join me?"

"No." Three voices in unison. I would have laughed in other circumstances.

We sat in silence, listening to Patrick taking exaggerated steps down the hallway, his boots stomping on the wooden floorboards. A minute later we heard a window slam shut.

"It's all good," he shouted. "The hall window had just blown open."

I relaxed a little, just as Kara and Zoe let out a yelp. The pointer started to slide again: Y…O…U

"This isn't funny, Kara," Zoe hissed through gritted teeth.

Kara's eyes followed the letters. "It's not me, Zoe. I swear."

A…R…E…A…L…L…L…I…A…R…S

I tried to keep up as it slid faster across the board.

Patrick returned and sat next to me on the rug. He slowly read out the new words as they formed:

"YOU...NEVER...LOVED...ME." He shook his head. "Louise?" he whispered, frightened eyes darting around the room.

"Don't be ridiculous." Kara took her hand away. "I don't like this. I think we should stop."

"Just one more question." Zoe kept her finger on the pointer.

I shook my head. "I'm with Kara. This is creepy. Please stop."

Patrick stood up as Zoe blurted out her question.

"Is the killer here just now?"

The fire cracked, flames dancing wildly.

I realised I was backing away from the table, sliding myself across the floor, trying to distance myself from the others.

The pointer twitched, then slowly scraped back to *Yes*.

Zoe and Kara took their hands away, as if they had been burnt.

I clambered to my feet, studying each of their faces intently. Slowly, the fear on Kara's face softened into an amused smile. Then her expression hardened as she turned to me.

My pulse throbbed in my neck as I registered the coldness in her eyes. There was no trace of humour as she said, "Well, you wanted to know, didn't you, Darcy?"

Every instinct was telling me to run. But where to? I stumbled to my feet, edging backwards. Two strong hands grabbed my arms. I whimpered as Patrick's breath tickled my neck.

"I told you a while back to stop sticking your nose in, Darcy."

"What are you doing? Stop it, Patrick." Zoe stood up, shaking her head.

As I felt Patrick's grip loosen, I elbowed him in the ribs, full force. He buckled.

I didn't stop to think as I half slid, half ran along the hall, grabbing at the torch and boots lying at the door. I nearly cried with relief when I saw the keys still in the door. I launched myself at them, my hands shaking so much that it took two attempts to click the lock open.

"Darcy, don't be stupid!" Kara was behind me. "We were just trying to scare you. You can't go out in that…"

I didn't stop. I flung the door open and the wind swept a sheet of rain into my face. I pulled the boots on and slammed the door shut behind me, fearing my heart might explode from my chest as I thundered down the muddy path into the darkness, *Run Run Run* raging in my head.

Chapter Twenty-One

I ran through the fields, the light from the torch only strong enough to illuminate the small section of grass in front of me. The boots were too big and I kept losing my footing, half lunging, half falling through the mud. The raging wind made it impossible to keep my hood up, leaving the rain to pound my face.

Don't turn round, don't turn round. I imagined Patrick and Kara jumping out from the shadows, pulling me back to the cabin. I struggled to breathe, unsure if it was the result of exhaustion or panic. The one sound I could hear above the howling of the wind was blood whooshing in my ears.

I swung the torch helplessly from side to side, staring into what seemed an endless dark stretch of nothing. I had no sense of where I was heading. My legs started to slow as my rational mind caught up. It was night. If I kept running blindly, I would get lost, with no hope of reaching any kind of shelter. The wind whipped my hair against my face. I stopped running and tentatively circled my torch around, looking back to see if I could make out the cabin. Needles stabbed at my retinas as my eyes struggled to stay open against the rain. I blinked as dots of light blurred in the distance.

I would die of hypothermia if I stayed out here. I had already lost feeling in my legs, numbed by rain seeping through my jeans like melting ice. I pictured the coldness in Kara's eyes, could still feel pain in my arms from Patrick's grip. If I went back there, what was going to happen? What were they playing at?

I tried to zone out, focusing on my breathing. One

deep breath in, one deep breath out. In….out… *Think, Darcy. Think*. My heart calmed as I thought back to Kara's parting words… *We were just trying to scare you*.

My eyes sprung open as a whoosh of air nearly knocked me off balance. Fingers dug into my wrist. I screamed, hitting out at the figure, a flash of light blinding me.

"Darcy, calm down, calm down," a voice shouted above the wind. I continued to lash out until my assailant backed off, lowering their torch.

I raised my own torch to illuminate the figure in red. Zoe pulled back the hood of her coat, her eyes fearful and relieved.

"Thank god. We thought we'd never find you." She pulled me to her in a hug, but I resisted, anger simmering over my fear.

"What the hell was that all about, back there?" I yelled.

She shook her head helplessly. "I'm sorry, it went too far. We thought it would be funny to try and scare you. Kara wasn't supposed to get so dramatic."

"Well it wasn't funny." I pushed her away. "I just want to go home."

Zoe grimaced as the wind buffeted her. She shrugged. "You can leave first thing in the morning. I'll get up early and walk you to the station. But we need to get back to the cabin, now, before this gets worse."

I hesitated, every part of my body trembling.

"Please, come on." Zoe tugged at my hand.

I relented and we ran side by side, torches illuminating a muddy trail back to the cabin. I was surprised at how far my adrenaline had carried me.

Two figures came into sight and I deftly side-stepped Patrick as he launched himself at me. He stumbled, grabbing at my arm.

"Get off me!" I whacked his arm with my torch.

"Ouch." He rubbed at his arm. "I'm sorry, Darcy. I was just happy to see you. We're sorry."

"Come on, we need to keep going." Zoe motioned for us to hurry. The light from her torch was starting to fade.

I kept my head lowered against the rain, pulling my hood over as far as it could go, keeping a tight grip on it. I was only aware that we had reached the cabin when I nearly ran into the back of Kara. The lights from inside shone with warmth. My body ached for comfort and safety. As we all fell through the door, dripping wet and shivering, Kara turned to me.

"We took it too far, Darcy. We just wanted you to back off a bit."

I stared at her. "Which suggests you're hiding something. But you know what, I really don't care anymore. I just want to go to bed and I'm leaving in the morning." I wriggled out of the soaking coat, letting it fall to the ground, and pulled off the boots, leaving a pool of water in the hall.

"At least have a hot drink before you go to bed," Zoe called after me.

I shook my head. "I'll be fine. Night." I ran up the stairs, my socks slipping against the wood and nearly sending me flying backwards. I rushed into the attic room, slamming the door shut. Body shaking, I slid down onto the floor and burst into tears.

*

Hours passed and I stared up at the wooden beams on the ceiling, pulling the quilt tighter around me as the wind continued to howl outside. Every once in a while, I cast nervous glances towards the door. I had propped a chair against it, realising deep down it would do little to hold the force of someone really wanting to enter. But it was what they did in movies.

I clicked my phone to check the time. Midnight. I would get up at six, shower and leave before anyone woke. I had no idea what time the buses started running, but decided I would walk to the station if I had to.

The tapping on the window started again. I burrowed further down under the covers, Zoe's words from earlier: *"You came tapping, tapping, at my chamber door... darkness there and nothing more."* So familiar. Where was that line from?

A flash of light flickered from my phone. I grabbed it, relieved when I saw, *Daniel Calling.*

"Hello?"

A crackling, then Daniel's voice was in my ear, *"I tried to call earlier – are you at the cabin? Are you okay?"*

"Yes," I whispered loudly. "But I'm leaving tomorrow..."

"...Christian called...don't trust..."

I gripped the phone closer to my ear, Daniel's voice dipping in and out. "Daniel, I can't hear you properly. You keep breaking up."

"...Mr Harris...coming to get you."

"What? Daniel?" More crackling then a beep and nothing. I tried to call him, but the bars kept disappearing. "Stupid phone." I held it high above my head, pointing it at the ceiling as if some magical phone mast would appear. What had he been trying to tell me? Was he trying to warn me not to trust Mr Harris? A chill ran up my legs. What if Daniel had discovered something about him? I thought about Mum at home, anxiety knotting my stomach.

I pieced together the picture I'd formed of Louise. Spoilt, beautiful, manipulative. She seemed to like to be the one in control. What if she had flirted with Mr Harris in class and he *had* started to invite her to his exhibitions? Maybe he ran her home one night, she tried to kiss him…then got annoyed when he rebuked her advances, and that's when she started to spread rumours?

But what if there was some truth to the rumours? What if she had threatened to expose the truth and Mr Harris had silenced her. He could have sneaked into the party in costume…

No. I shook my head. Christian seemed so certain that Mr Harris was a good guy. But he hadn't stayed with his mum once Christian had been put away. Julia had been almost hysterical at Mr Harris's exhibition, accusing him of not responding to her emails. Why had he suddenly stopped seeing her? Because he had got what he wanted? Because he had made sure her son was put away for something Mr Harris had done?

I spoke to my phone like a mad woman, as if Daniel was still on the other end. "Daniel, if you've found out something sinister about him, you'd better goddamn look after Mum until I'm home."

Chapter Twenty-Two

I woke with a jolt, glancing first at the chair – still in place – then at the time. Six thirty. I'd slept in. It was a miracle I'd slept at all. I detangled myself from the quilt, my body on fire with the layers I had piled on last night to stop shivering. As I pulled off my jumper, I realised the wind had stopped howling and rain was no longer battering the roof. I decided to skip the shower and changed quickly, tummy growling, reminding me that, with all of the previous night's drama, I hadn't eaten much. There would be food in the kitchen that I could grab on my way out.

I checked to see if I had a signal on my phone yet. Nothing. The desperation to talk to Daniel urged me on. I pulled on my muddy trainers and winced when a cold dampness seeped into the soles of my feet. I could steal the boots again, but the ones last night had nearly made me fall over. Wishing I'd brought my hairdryer I started opening drawers, hoping Zoe had stashed one in the room. I searched the bedside cabinet; nothing. Then I opened the wardrobe and ran a hand along the top shelf. My knuckles grazed something solid – a box. I hesitated, knowing I should hurry, but curiosity got the better of me. I pulled the box down and traced a finger along the intricate wooden carvings. I opened the lid, surprised to find a small stack of letters inside, tied with a red ribbon.

My heart lurched when I lifted the bundle. I recognised the artistic handwriting and prison stamp. It could easily be my stack of letters I was staring at, but these were addressed to Zoe.

Hands shaking, I untied the ribbon and slid out the

first letter. A sketch of Zoe fluttered to the ground; delicate pencil lines capturing her elfin features with a startling accuracy. I marvelled at the depth of emotion in her eyes – as if the artist knew her intimately and had glimpsed her soul.

My finger traced the heart drawn around the image. *The person who drew this loved her.* The thought hit me like a slap across the face as I unfolded the letter.

Dear Zoe,

It's so hard not being able to talk properly when you visit. I miss you so much. How's your mum, and Roo?

In answer to your question – regret is too strong a word. You keep asking me, so I want you to understand: I will keep my promise to you.

I had a dream about you again last night. We were in the park and people were running past the gates, dressed as skeletons, shouting and laughing. Then silence; just me and you, sitting side by side. It reminded me of that afternoon – when we kissed for the first time.

In the dream you held my hand as we lay on the roundabout. We spun round and round and you kept shouting, "Make a wish." I leaned over and kissed you and I swear when I woke up I could taste your strawberry lip balm. For a few blissful waking moments, I imagined I was back there with you.

I don't think you realise how you made me feel. I never thought you'd be interested in a weirdo loser like me. I'd liked you for such a long time – I never told you that. I wish I had.

When we worked on the science project together, I loved our conversations about life, books, horror films, music. A light switched on in my brain when I was around you. Like you really listened to me, and got me.

I'm sorry I ran away the afternoon we were finishing up the project, when you told me how grateful you were that I had taken on so much extra work when your mum got really ill. When you laid your hand on mine, I panicked. I was nervous. I didn't want to mess things up.

When you ignored me the next day in school, not even looking my way when you walked past with Louise and Kara, I thought I'd blown it big time. I thought we'd never speak again because the science project had ended too. Then you approached me in the park that afternoon, and you know the rest...

If I could have three wishes right now they would be:

I wish I wasn't in here. I wish I was with you. I wish we had never gone to that stupid party.

Love, Christian

The words blurred in front of me. Christian and Zoe. Together. Kissing. *Keeping secrets from everyone.* Or was it just me who didn't know, who was being played for a fool? I swallowed back tears. If Christian had been keeping their relationship a secret, what else might he have lied about? My brain tried to make connections, but all I could hear was a taunting voice: *You never should have trusted any of them.*

Hands shaking, I opened another letter.

Hey Zoe,

It took me a while to write this – I want to find words to try to make you feel better but everything sounds so lame. I can't even imagine how difficult the funeral must have been. I thought about you all day. You don't need to apologise for not writing so much. I get it – you've got to look after Roo now. It sounds like she's a handful. Everything in here is OK. It's getting better – really. It's looking more positive that I could put in an appeal. Don't worry about me, okay? And I don't hate you.

A bang downstairs made me jump. I paused, holding my breath, listening for other sounds. Silence, apart from the clock ticking on the wall.

I turned my attention back to the letters, lines jumping out at me:

I will keep my promise to you.

I wish we had never gone to that stupid party.

What exactly had he promised Zoe? What really happened that night? I needed to know.

I ripped open another letter.

Hey Zoe,

Long time no speak. You sounded a bit angry in your letter. There's nothing for you to worry about – Darcy seems okay. I know it's weird, like she's obsessed with my case, but it must be strange moving to a village that's had so much media coverage. I think I'd be curious too. Plus she's been hanging around with Daniel, so he's probably been talking about me. I'm glad she's befriended him – he seems a lot happier these days. I think you'd like Darcy if you gave her a chance. It sounds like she's going through stuff just now too. And you'd also like Daniel. They'd be good friends to you.

I don't know why you still want to hang around with Patrick after what he did. I really need you to tell the police that part – then they'll know I didn't hit Louise. Patrick's parents are wealthy enough they could get the best legal support. It might be enough to get me my appeal, to argue they didn't find enough conclusive evidence. Would you be able to do that for me? I know you said you're scared in case they find out more, but I'm kinda scared when I think of getting moved out of here when I turn twenty-one. Anyway, it was good to hear from you. It's been too long. I hope you're okay. How's Roo? Has your dad been around much?

A door slammed downstairs and I folded the letters back into their envelopes, shoving them into my backpack. I gathered up the last of my things and zipped up my coat, no longer caring about my sodden trainers. Every inch of my body was screaming, *Get out of this house.* It was Patrick who hit Louise? Did he stab her too?

As I crept down the attic stairs, the smell of toast rose to greet me. My heart sank. Surely they couldn't all be up this early.

A lamp was on in the hallway and I could see light from under the kitchen door. The living room was in darkness, the fire settled into embers. I crept across the hall, hoping no floorboards would squeak. The lamp didn't extend much light along the hall and I could only just make out the front door. I reached up for a torch, but the hooks beside the door were empty. It should soon be light anyway. I reached down to turn the key, only for my hand to brush against an empty lock. *Damn it.* I tried the handle, rattling it in frustration, forgetting my attempt at silence.

I jumped as the kitchen door squeaked open, illuminating Zoe in its frame. I studied her face, trying to figure out what might be going on inside her head. Was she angry because I was paying Christian so much attention, or because I was digging for the truth?

Zoe motioned me over, handing me a plate of toast and a cup of tea. I took them gratefully, joining her at the breakfast table, relieved to find no Patrick or Kara.

"They're still fast asleep," Zoe whispered, as if she could read my mind. "I heard Patrick snoring. There's no chance of them getting up for another good few hours."

As I ate, I noticed the set of keys and two torches lying beside Zoe's bag on the counter, remembering with dread her saying she would walk me to the station. I would rather go alone now and get far away from them all.

Last night I thought Kara and Patrick were the ringleaders, but Christian's letters suggested there was much more to the story. Zoe knew things that she was refusing to disclose to the police.

"What was that all about last night?" I said, watching Zoe's expression carefully.

"It was a stupid joke." Zoe smiled apologetically. "It was Kara's idea. She just wants everyone to forget that night. Her and Patrick had to endure a lot of scrutiny, people poking their noses into all aspects of their lives. Her mum didn't cope well with the experience – she drank constantly. It brings back a lot of bad memories for Kara."

"And what about you?"

Zoe blinked, frowning. "What do you mean?"

"I just got the feeling last night that there was something you were all trying to hide." My mug was slippy in my hands as I watched her expression carefully. Was I being stupid, still trying to push things? Kara and Patrick were so protective of Zoe. Maybe I was obsessing over nothing and Christian truly was guilty. Maybe they didn't want Zoe being upset by it all again. But that didn't explain the comment about Patrick hitting Louise.

Zoe sighed. "I think you should leave it, Darcy." She glanced at her watch. "Let's get going. I think the buses to the station start running just after seven. I'll take you the route up to the road."

I hesitated. "You don't have to walk me, it's okay. I can remember the way, I think."

Zoe made a face. "Really? You didn't look like you had a clue last night. Anyway, I got up especially, come on."

I drained the last of my tea and Zoe checked the torches had power before we set off into the darkness once more.

As we tramped through the fields, the moon shone a dull blue hue in the sky. The grass was still wet from the previous night's storm, but the calm air made it a much easier trek. The more distance we put between us and the cabin, the more I relaxed. Each step was a step closer to home. I would be able to phone Daniel when I was on the bus and I was sure he would agree to meet me from the train at the other end. I kept my distance from Zoe, scrutinising her every move. I thought back to Christian's letter and his suggestion that I could be a friend to her. I'd often felt like she wanted to open up to me; maybe I should try to talk to her about Christian.

Zoe slowed to a stop. I lowered my torch.

"What's wrong?" I asked.

She shone her torch to the patch of field in front. "It looks too marshy to get past this way. If we detour around the trees ahead and climb up the path, it will lead us back round to the road."

"Okay, lead the way," I said, grateful that Zoe had agreed to walk with me after all. It would have been difficult for me to navigate alone in the dark. I was unfamiliar with the area and realised I had no real concept of where we were.

Branches scraped at my legs as we fought our way through a dense stretch of woodland. I stumbled over roots, convinced that a distant owl's hooting was directed at me, mocking my lack of outdoor finesse. I struggled to keep up with Zoe, who darted through the winding paths with confidence. She motioned for me to follow her up a rocky ridge. My fingernails dug into dirt as I struggled to stop myself from slipping, still gripping the torch with my other hand. I kept my mouth firmly shut, and half closed my eyes, as Zoe kicked back clouds of dust and rubble.

As we ascended, my phone started to vibrate in my pocket, messages finally finding their way through.

"Have you got reception?" Zoe turned her head in surprise.

"Sounds like it." I started to reach into my jacket.

"You should wait till we reach the top, it's getting

steeper," Zoe called. "You'll get better reception up there anyway, with the phone masts."

I picked up my pace, but felt more vibrations. Curiosity got the better of me. I paused at a section of slope where I could balance both feet on a rocky ledge, pulling out my phone and sliding the torch into my pocket to free both hands so I could open the messages more quickly. I ignored the ones from Mum (I could guess the wrath of those) and Fee, focusing instead on Daniel's. He'd sent one after we'd got cut off last night:

Christian called and told me that the girl who has been visiting is Zoe. He seemed a bit anxious when I mentioned you'd gone to the cabin with them all. I don't think you should trust her. Me and Mr Harris are coming to get you. Just stay at the cabin. We'll come first thing tomorrow.

I reached for the torch, hands shaking. Why would Christian be anxious? My mind was racing, running back through the letters. *I don't have any regrets as such...I stand by my promise to you.* What had Christian promised?

I shone the torch up towards Zoe. Her pace was slowing now she was ascending the steepest part of the climb. I scrambled up behind her, moving fast, desperate to reach the road.

Zoe's back arched as she stretched to pull herself to the top of the ridge. Her jacket rode up at the back and, as I moved behind, the light from my torch illuminated her crow tattoo. My eyes traced the large beak.

'...*you came tapping, tapping at my chamber*

door...darkness there and nothing more.'

The day I sat beside Zoe in English...when Mrs Clark had recited gothic poetry...*The Raven.* I realised that Zoe's tattoo was a raven, not a crow – that she had been quoting from the poem. The poem by *Edgar* Allan Poe.

Distracted by this realisation, I stumbled. As my foot slipped, Zoe turned and grabbed my arm, dragging me up to the peak.

As I scrambled to my feet, Zoe's face was so pale it almost shone in the darkness, her black messy hair blowing in the breeze. She was a raven poised for flight...or attack. Why would she have posted so many incriminating things about Christian in forums if they were in love?

I shivered, a creeping sense of danger gripping my bones. I tried to get my bearings. My stomach dipped when I looked down into a deep gully, an endless pit of darkness below us. Another line from *The Raven* popped into my head, *'Deep into that darkness peering, long I stood there, wondering, fearing...'*

The traffic noise was a distant hum. We still had another climb before we reached safety.

Zoe turned to check on me. She frowned. "What's wrong? You look like you've seen a ghost."

She stepped closer and I instinctively moved back. The desire – the need – to know the truth gnawed at me, fighting with my desire to keep safe.

"We don't have far to go. The road is just up ahead." Zoe pointed to the steep grassy verge above. "Think you can make it okay?"

I nodded, not taking my eyes off her.

She tilted her head questioningly. "What's wrong, Darcy? Why are you looking at me like that?"

"I'm not sure, Edgar."

A flicker of surprise and anger flashed in Zoe's eyes.

"You posted those things about Christian on those forums?" I shook my head. "I don't understand. Why you would do that when you...?"

"When I what?" she prompted.

"Why would you want him found guilty when you...love him?" I whispered.

Zoe stared at me, the colour draining from her face. A mix of emotions sparked in her eyes: panic, fear...sadness? "Did Christian tell you that? What else did he tell you?"

I shook my head, edging back, conscious of not wanting to move too close to the gully.

"Why do you always have to ask so many questions? We kept telling you to stop." Zoe's face hardened. "I always thought if anyone was going to figure things out, it would be Daniel. That Christian would crack and tell him. But then you came along, poking your nose in."

My phone was heavy in my hand. I pressed to call Daniel, raising the handset to my ear. I screamed as Zoe slapped my hand hard, sending the phone spinning from my grasp. I grabbed for it, but watched helplessly as it soared through the air, disappearing over the edge into the gully.

"Why did you do that?" I tried to back away, wondering if I could make it safely down the route we had just ascended.

"Have you told Christian that I'm Edgar?" Zoe's voice wavered.

I shook my head, "No, it was when I saw your tattoo..."

Zoe absentmindedly touched the base of her back. "You're so smart aren't you, Darcy?" Her voice was dripping with sarcasm. "I bet you can't wait to run away and tell Christian I stirred up all the hate online. After all he's done for me, it'll kill him."

I flinched at the word kill.

"Did Christian tell you it was an accident? That Louise provoked me?" Zoe's eyes were wild as she took a step towards me. "She was threatening to send photos to my dad – told me that he'd started to chat to her online after flirting with her at our parents' parties while my mum was lying ill in bed at home, crippled with pain. My family was already falling apart, and she wanted to cause even more destruction with her stupid attention-seeking."

I stared at her in shock, wanting to scream that Christian hadn't told me anything. I held up my hands, attempting a calming motion, like the police on television when confronted with aggressive criminals. "I'm sure you didn't mean it. I know you would never hurt anyone intentionally, Zoe. That's not you."

Zoe laughed bitterly, her eyes cold and emotionless. "You don't know anything about me, Darcy. You don't know what I'm capable of."

I screamed as she lunged at me and the weight of her body knocked me off my feet. My arms flayed, hands grabbing at the material of Zoe's coat as I fell backwards into the pit of darkness.

Chapter Twenty-Three

I was still falling: *down, down, down.*

Yet…

My eyes flickered open. My head was spinning but I realised I was lying down. It was only my body trying to persuade me that I was still falling.

I tried to comprehend where I was. So much darkness closing around me. The smell of damp earth. The feel of a cold surface traced under my finger. Mortuary-slab cold.

I attempted to sit up, but flames of pain shot through me, curling up from my toes, ripping through my back and spreading to my arm. *My arm!* The bones felt distorted and loose. I squeezed my eyes shut, nausea hitting me in waves. Someone was calling my name.

No. Just leave me. I want to sleep.

"Darcy? Are you alive?"

A scream raged silently through me as a hand touched my leg. A pale face peered through the shadows. Edgar. *Zoe.*

"Don't touch me." *Get away, get away.* But my body wouldn't move.

"You're alive." She sounded relieved.

Why are you relieved when you tried to kill me?

"Are we in hell?" I murmured.

"We're in the gully; a ledge stopped our fall. I think I've broken my leg. Are you okay?"

The fire burned up my arm. "What do you care? You pushed me."

A sob caught in Zoe's throat. "I'm sorry. I panicked…"

Her voice was a wail, words spinning on the wind, flying up, up, up…a raven, a demon, *a killer.*

Fingers tapped my cheek. *No, no, go away, let me sleep.*

"Darcy, please. You have to stay awake. I honestly don't want you to die."

The darkness took my hand, pulling me, asking me to dance.

"HELP US. PLEASE. SOMEBODY HELP US."

I flinched at Zoe's screams. *Yes, please help us! Save us, Daniel. Please!*

"Talk to me, Darcy. You need to stay conscious."

"No, you talk to me. I want the truth. Tell me your story." *Do you still care, Darcy? Now you're lying here dying, does it matter? Yes. Yes. Yes.*

Hesitation, an intake of breath, then, "Fine. You're half-delusional anyway. You want a story, here's my story." Zoe lay beside me, whimpering in pain as she tried to position her leg. "The day of the party, Louise saw me and Christian kissing in the park..."

I listened as Zoe continued, images flashing as I pictured it all playing out. The taunts from Louise as she asked if Christian was a good kisser, *He's a bit weird, Zoe. Not really your type. I wonder if he likes blondes too, like your dad.* I listened to Zoe's impression of Louise. *Your dad told me I remind him so much of your mum when they first met – vivacious, beautiful...*

"Can you imagine how that made me feel?" Zoe's voice wavered. "I was worried she was going to start stupid rumours, like she did with Mr Harris. My mum was already going through enough. Rumours in our village can catch fire. If the Marshalls thought there was a glimmer of truth in it they would destroy my

Dad."

Zoe described searching for Christian at the party, thinking he hadn't shown up. Then she spotted his bag, found his sketchbook, and flicked through pages upon pages of sketches of Louise. *Beautiful, manipulative, scheming. Always capturing boys' attention.*

"I found Christian upstairs, hurrying out of a bedroom. His arm was bleeding and he was upset." Zoe's voice hardened. "I wish I'd just left then, with him, but I got distracted by something else...then I could hear shouting from the bedroom – Louise and Patrick. Patrick was drunk, calling her a tease – '*Why were you dancing with that loser? Why do you always have to flirt with everyone?*' When Patrick slapped Louise hard across the face, I should have intervened, asked her if she was okay. But I just stood and watched, thinking she had it coming to her. Who did she think she was, flirting and dancing with Christian? The music was still spinning on the turntable. All I could think was, *You spoiled brat.*"

An image of Patrick, his breath smelling of whisky, his fingers digging into my skin, voice menacing, *I think you should leave well alone.* Had they murdered Louise together? I struggled to keep my eyes open, Zoe's voice echoing.

"I saw the shock on Patrick's face - his grovelling apology - but Louise was hysterical, shouting for him to leave. He begged me not to tell anyone. I told him to go. Louise hugged me, with her tears soaking my dress as I listened to her whine on and on about Patrick, how he didn't really know or understand her... whereas Christian had danced with her and made her happy.

"Then Louise was all smiles, as if nothing had

happened. '*Is my make-up running? I must be a right mess. Be a sweetheart, Zoe and hand me my phone.*' Always so patronising, always thinking she could push me around. Sweet, pathetic little Zoe. And then she started to show me the selfies she'd taken - pouting, skimpily dressed. Laughing at me as she said, '*I think I'll send this one to your dad, do you think he'll like it?*'"

Zoe's body convulsed beside me, tears catching in the back of her throat. She described a glint of metal under an album cover, the curve of a knife. Christian's knife from his costume.

She tried to grab Louise's phone, begged her to delete the photos. *No, no, no.*

The knife plunged in deep.

"Blood was seeping into the carpet so I dragged her out onto the balcony. Christian came back for his stupid lighter. He should never have come back," Zoe whispered. "The look on his face… I was in shock. I told him there had been an accident and he wasn't to go out on the balcony. That Louise had attacked *me* in a rage because I wanted to stop her calling the police about Patrick. And Christian believed me. Because everyone knew what Louise was like."

My head spun as anger flared inside me. "How could you let Christian get put away for a murder *you* committed? How could you do that? And why did he let you?"

"He understood that I couldn't leave my mum, or Roo. My dad has never been any use…he's hardly here. I knew mum didn't have long and Roo was only thirteen. I was worried about what might happen to her. I couldn't let anything happen to her."

Stupid, naive Christian. A sadness swept over me. "How could you ruin his life like that, when he loves

227

you?"

Zoe sobbed. "I didn't think it would ever go that far. Neither of us thought there was enough conclusive evidence. I thought some of Patrick's DNA would show up with the cut on Louise's lip, and that there would be enough doubt so that neither of them would go down. But the police kept questioning Christian. We…Patrick and I…we were wearing gloves with our costumes, it prevented fingerprints from showing up. It always came back to Christian, his knife, his fingerprints in the bedroom, on door handles. The case was high profile, so they were desperate to find the killer. I had to be sure, even if Christian broke, no one would believe him. I didn't think he would keep my secret. And then I realised how easy it was to distort the truth online."

So many secrets, so many lies, so much betrayal.

"And I was right, I knew Christian wouldn't stay silent forever. He told you."

"You're wrong. Christian *did* keep your secret," I whispered. "I found your letters. He didn't break his promise to you."

Zoe sobbed beside me.

Distorted images danced in front of my eyes: a white ghost drowning in a sea of red, shouting to me, telling me she could rest now that I had found the truth. She grabbed my hand and pulled me under.

Chapter Twenty-Four

"She's waking up, her eyes are opening."

A familiar voice, warm, *safe*. A hand brushed my forehead. I opened my eyes, flinching at the sunlight piercing the sky. A face smiled down at me. *Daniel.*

"It's okay. You're safe now."

Another familiar voice. Mr Harris.

"You found me." Tears of relief stung my eyes. I tried to blink them away.

The landscape of fields and trees was dipping up and down. The backs of two men were in front of me, the heads of two other strangers behind…above, looking down on me. It took me a moment to realise that they were carrying me. Stretcher-bearers.

How long had we been trapped down there, Zoe and I? I strained to look ahead, unable to lift my head much. I could see another stretcher in front – and hear a commotion as Zoe struggled. "Let me go. I don't need to be carried. Just let me go."

Patrick and Kara walked solemnly beside her, holding hands.

"It was him, it was him all along. It was Patrick who murdered Louise."

Patrick shook his head sadly. "Stop it, Zoe; it's over." *Did he know?*

Zoe slumped back onto her stretcher, muttering to herself as Patrick stroked her head. I guessed he really did think of her as a little sister.

Daniel stepped closer to my stretcher, concern etched across his face. "Are you okay, Darcy?"

I nodded, wanting to reach out and take his hand, but my arm – which I had little doubt was broken –

was in a sling, and the rest of my body had been wrapped tight inside the blanket. I motioned for him to bend his head so I could whisper in his ear. "It wasn't Christian, he didn't do it."

"I know." Daniel squeezed my knee. "I know."

*

I spread all of the letters, forum clippings and photographs out across the living room table. I picked up a photograph of Christian, remembering that afternoon in my old school when I first heard about his case. I had become so entranced with his story, so drawn to him. Zoe must have cast a similar spell over Christian, except hers had created a stronger bind; he had fallen in love – fallen hard.

"How could he be so stupid?" I crumpled up the photos, throwing them at the bin with my good arm.

Mum sat down across from me, sliding a mug of steaming hot chocolate across the table. She laid a hand on mine. She had resisted endlessly repeating, 'I told you so', which I realised was very restrained seeing as she had warned me for months to give up on my obsession. I hadn't ever considered the danger I might put myself in.

"Well, you said he fell in love. First love can be really powerful; it can entice you with its magic and allure." Mum smiled ruefully. "When I first met your dad, I was only eighteen, and he spoke so little during our first six months together I think he allowed me to superimpose every fictional character I had ever romanticised onto his handsome six-foot frame. I was besotted – all common sense went out the window."

I listened with curiosity. I knew Mum and Dad had met when really young, but I hadn't paid much attention to their story.

"Not that we didn't love each other for real – we

did, very much. But I don't think we were ever truly compatible, ever fully at home with one another. To be honest, Darcy, I'm not the easiest person to live with."

I snorted and Mum laughed.

"I think I drove your sensible father a little bit bonkers really. He did well to put up with me for so long."

I took a deep breath. "Do you love Mr Harris?"

Mum looked at me in surprise, as if she hadn't considered this. "It's early days, Darcy. All I want to focus on just now is making sure you're okay. *Are you okay?* I feel like I stopped knowing you for a while there." I folded the letters closed, wanting to explain my motivations but not fully understanding them myself. Her grip tightened on my hand. "I was so scared when Timothy and Daniel rushed off in such a panic to the cabin. What exactly happened up there? Are you sure you're okay?"

"You know I always love to solve a good mystery, Mum." *I just didn't realise I would nearly get killed in the process.* "I'm sorry I lied to you."

"I was imagining all sorts, knowing you'd gone off to that cabin in the middle of nowhere. That girl, Zoe, sounds like one very disturbed young lady."

"Mm," I mumbled, wondering just how much Mr Harris had elaborated. We had agreed not to tell Mum the whole story of my 'adventure', choosing to let Mum believe my broken arm and various cuts had been sustained in a less dramatic fall.

"You know your dad was really worried too. He misses you."

I didn't look up.

Mum stood up and half-hugged me from behind, carefully avoiding my broken arm and numerous bruises, pressing her cheek against mine.

I closed my eyes, basking in the safety of home, my thoughts turning to Zoe. It was impossible not to feel some sympathy for her, even if she had nearly killed me. She had been desperate not to be taken away from her mum during her final days, and equally desperate not to leave Roo on her own. I could understand that need to hold on to family. But the way she had manipulated Christian, let him believe she'd done it in self-defence. I couldn't shake the image of her plunging in a knife, knowingly, purposely. I shivered.

Mum ruffled my hair. "I'm going to have a bath. We should go out for dinner tomorrow, just me and you?"

"Yeah. I'd like that." I smiled, watching her skip down the hall.

I picked up my new phone, scrolling through the contacts, thinking about what she'd said about Dad. I held my breath as I hit Call.

"Sweetheart." A flood of relief flowed through me as I heard the cheer in my dad's voice.

I bit my lip to stop from crying as I felt my throat close up.

"Sorry I haven't called much, Dad. How are you?"

"Oh, love. I'm sorry too. I've…I've never been very good at this, you know. But I want you to know, I love you very much, and you know, I'm always going to make sure you're both taken care of. Okay? Mum was telling me you've been through a bit the past few weeks, so I hope you don't mind, but I booked a flight to come and visit this weekend. Is that okay?"

"Yes." I nodded, tears rolling down my cheeks.

I looked down at a photograph of Christian, a rare one of him smiling at the camera.

As my tears blurred his smile, I ran a finger along the blotches.

I hoped that someday soon Christian would get to see his dad too.

After the Party

They could hear the rage of the bonfire as they approached, flames stretching into the black sky. A group of college students were gathered in a circle nearby, so off their faces that they barely noticed Christian and Zoe's arrival. A couple of boys were on the swings, their hysteria increasing the higher they flew.

Zoe threw her dress, gloves and Christian's white sheet onto the fire, grabbing his hand tightly, squeezing in reassurance. It was going to be okay. No one would find out. They stood side by side, watching the clothes burn, shivering beneath coats that smelled of someone else's perfume and aftershave, stolen from a pile of belongings at the party.

"I wish I'd found my bag." Christian shook his head, wanting to wipe any trace of his existence at the party. He reached into the pocket of his jeans, relieved he had found his lighter. He turned it over in his hand, thinking back to Zoe's panic - her concern for Roo. This lighter felt like the only connection he still had with his dad, Charlie Henderson. From what he knew of Zoe's dad, he couldn't imagine he would stick around for long to look after her sister and mum if Zoe was put away.

Christian watched the flames dance, illuminating Zoe's face. Her eyes were bright with a feverish fear. He tensed when he saw the pain in them.

"I'm so scared," she whispered.

Christian clasped her hand, intertwining his fingers with hers. "It's going to be okay. I won't let anything happen to you."

"Promise me?" She turned her face up to his.

"I promise." And in that moment, he knew he would do anything to protect her.

Young Offenders' Unit: Now

As Christian followed the boy in front, the rhythm of his steps lulled him into a calmer state. He turned his face up to the sky, catching rain in his mouth. He squeezed his eyes shut at the memory of the pain in his mum's voice earlier that morning.

"Why, son? How could you have put me through this?"

"I'm sorry." The phone had shaken in his hand. "I thought Mr Harris would look after you. Zoe's mum was dying. She had to be there for her, and for her little sister. Her dad's never there."

"We could have made sure she was okay. We could have looked after her sister." His mum's voice broke and Christian felt sick. *"Anything would have been better than this. Don't you see that?"*

"I'm sorry. I loved her. I love her, Mum. I couldn't abandon her. I know what that feels like. She promised she'd come forward with more information, to help my appeal..." Christian paused, his mum's silence hitting him full force, the realisation that in protecting Zoe he had abandoned his mum. He had buried that thought, but it had resurfaced whenever she had visited, and now it was something he would always regret.

His heart twisted at the thought of Zoe. When Daniel had mentioned the threats Darcy had started to receive from someone called Edgar, the memory of the forum postings had flooded back to Christian. At first he had thought Edgar must be Patrick, but he recalled more recent visits from Zoe when she had seemed overly interested in Darcy's curiosity about the case. Then there had been the anger in Zoe's letters when he had mentioned that Darcy was writing to him. It had been more than jealousy. He had started to piece together the cutting realisation that Zoe had been spinning all the lies. Had she ever even loved him?

Christian stomped across the concrete paths of the outdoor area, one foot in front of the other, boots splashing in puddles. Guilt and betrayal pulled at his gut and at his heart.

The rain stopped and a cool breeze circled him. He looked up at the sky, grey clouds parting to reveal a thread of sunshine.

Freedom. He could taste it in the air. It was near now, and it made his mouth water.

He had the rest of his life to make things right with his mum and with everyone else.

Chapter Twenty-Five

"There, all good." Kara smiled in approval before swivelling her chair round so that I could admire her work in the mirror.

I marvelled at how she had managed to find my cheekbones. I had been surprised when Kara started to message me, giving me updates about what I was missing at school. I knew she felt guilty, and she asked to do my make-up when I'd mentioned I was venturing out later to see Daniel. I told her on the condition she didn't over-do it. I knew I'd probably end up rubbing half of it off on the way to his, but I didn't want to hurt Kara's feelings when I knew it was her way of trying to reach out.

"Your lips look very kissable in that shade of strawberry crush," she smirked mischievously.

I watched as my face in the mirror turned an even brighter shade than strawberry crush. "I'd better get going."

"Okay, have a fun afternoon. See you at school on Monday?"

"Yeah." I wiggled my hand, indicating the plaster was now off. I paused, not missing the lull of sadness in Kara's voice. "I know it's hard, knowing Zoe won't be coming back. But at least they're trying to help her, not just locking her up."

Kara shrugged. "I'm not convinced that a mental health unit is going to be much better."

As I turned to leave, Kara touched my arm.

"Hey, Darcy. I am sorry you know, about everything. We didn't realise the full story. I knew how vindictive Louise could be; I just never realised

Zoe could be too." She looked ashamed. "We didn't realise Christian had nothing to do with it – that he covered for Zoe like that. Zoe never told us what really happened that night; she refused to talk about it. But she let us believe they were in it together and we felt so protective of her…"

"Yeah, I know. It's okay." I hesitated at the door. "Doesn't it bother you that Patrick hit Louise?"

Kara's head snapped up, face flushing. "Of course, it makes me mad, and…disappointed in him. He's never hurt me, but we're spending some time apart just now. You know he's having to go to anger management classes, that it was classed as assault?"

I hadn't known. But I was glad. The way Zoe had described that scene unsettled me.

Kara shifted in her chair. "You know Patrick's family life isn't as perfect as it looks. I'm not excusing what he did, but his parents have a toxic relationship."

I nodded, thinking back to the night I saw him crying and his comments about his parents arguing. I didn't need Kara to spell it out for me.

On my way down the main stairs, I heard the entrance door to the flats slam shut. I smiled in surprise when Mr Harris appeared, arms laden with a massive bouquet of flowers.

"Hey, Mr H. Been a while since I've seen you around here."

"Oh, hi Darcy." He looked sheepish when he saw me staring at the flowers. "Do you think your Mum will think this is overkill?"

I shook my head. "Nah. Mum likes overkill."

"Did you have a good time with your dad the other weekend?"

"I did." I smiled, realising the flowers might be a

reaction to Dad being back on the scene a lot more lately. "It was good to get some alone time with him."

Mr Harris's face relaxed at the word 'alone'.

"Are you off out?"

"Yeah, just heading to Daniel's."

"Oh, good. Say hi to him."

I turned to leave, then paused when I sensed Mr Harris's hesitation.

"Darcy, I want you to know that I always thought Christian was innocent. I suspected he was covering for someone. He nearly told me one afternoon, just before his trial. But then he changed his mind, and backtracked, refusing to admit that he had even alluded to it. I struggled with that suspicion for so long. It affected my relationship with his mother, because I wanted to say something but didn't know how I could. Would it be worse for her, suggesting her son had put her through unnecessary pain?"

I smiled in understanding. "At least the truth came out eventually."

He nodded sadly, waving me on my way.

I felt a surge of excitement and happiness as I climbed the hill to Daniel's. I dismissed it as relief; that I could start to enjoy my life in Rowantree and have fun hanging out with Daniel, playing pool.

I paused at the open garage door, watching as Daniel chalked his cue.

"Hey." I smiled with enthusiasm.

"Hey." Daniel glanced at me, then went back to chalking his cue.

A part of me deflated, disappointed that he seemed aloof. I unzipped my bag and laid a letter on the table.

"This came in the post. I wanted to wait to open it with you today. I recognise the handwriting – it's from Christian."

Daniel eyed the letter then went back to arranging the table. "If it's addressed to you, I don't think he'd want me hearing any of it."

I frowned at his tone. "I don't think he'd mind. Have you heard from him?"

"He phoned the other week, said he'll be in hiding for a bit what with the renewed media attention. I think he was worried he might get done for perjury but he never lied under oath because all he did was deny his own guilt, and they never put him on the stand. Though he did technically pervert the course of justice, or whatever the term was, defeat justice I think he said, by covering Zoe's actions, but he's already done time. I think officials didn't want any more negative media coverage."

I was conscious of Daniel's tense body language. "I know you're angry with him, but he did it for the right reasons."

Daniel shrugged. "I'm sure he'll be very appreciative of everything you've done for him."

Was he *jealous*? "Yeah, well. I'm sure some of his 'fans' will be the happiest ones. I was just a curious sleuth. My biggest fascination in all of this was to solve the mystery." I caught Daniel's eye. "Truly."

A half-smile tugged at his mouth as he worked his way round the pool table.

A warm glow spread through me as he moved closer.

"Come on, let me show you how this is done. Are you sure your arm is fully healed?"

"Hmm, I'm not sure. I might not play very well."

I tried my best to act nonchalant as he helped me position the cue. I omitted to tell him that I was a brilliant player and that my arm felt completely fine. I pulled back, ready to take my shot.

"By the way you look really pretty," he whispered in my ear, knocking me off course.

I stumbled, watching as the 8 ball spun across the table.

Daniel touched my arm, steadying me.

"I've got you," he said.

I smiled up at him. "Yes, you do."

Dear Darcy,

I'm not sure where to start with this letter. I just want to write to you to say thanks for everything and thanks for believing in me at a time when not a lot of people did. I think that's what I've struggled with the most during this whole experience – the way people in the community and strangers online believed the worst of me.

I know it might take a while for you to understand why I didn't just tell everyone the truth, why I chose to protect Zoe. And I know it's going to take a while for people to forgive me for my part in all of this. I'm starting to realise that Zoe wasn't who I thought she was, and that's a whole other struggle.

I guess all I can say is that sometimes it's easy to see life in black and white when it's always so much more. I'm glad you chose to look for the grey bits in between.

I hope we can be proper friends one day.

Later,

Christian Henderson

The Party: Scene Four

"Oh my god, oh my god," Roo retched and dropped her grip, Louise's leg sliding then smacking off the ground.

Zoe tensed, holding Louise tight under the arms, trying not to look at the blood. Roo was shaking and on the edge. She had to keep her calm.

"Roo. We need to get her outside. The rain will wash away evidence. Move." They laid her body in the middle of the balcony, Roo falling down onto her knees, crying beside Louise, shaking her head.

"I didn't mean it, Zo. When she was showing us those photos, saying she was going to send them to dad and teasing you about Christian. I just got so mad with her. She always humiliates everyone. What do we do? *What do we do?*"

Zoe heard a noise behind them in the bedroom. Her stomach plummeted as she looked at her sister, crumpled on the ground, a protective instinct driving her forward. Zoe grabbed Roo's arm, hauling her up, her voice calm and measured.

"You need to get out of here. Climb down from the balcony. You run home and hide your clothes. We'll get rid of them later. Have a shower and go to bed. You were never here, in this room, got it?"

Roo's bottom lip trembled. Zoe heard a voice call out. *Christian.* Her heart sank.

"He saw me earlier. In the hall…," Roo started to protest.

Zoe pressed a finger against her sister's lips to silence her. "He doesn't know you're still here. I'll handle this. Now, go."

Zoe stood very still, watching to make sure Roo didn't fall in her shocked, drunken state. Then she turned to face the balcony door which lay ajar, light streaming out from the bedroom. A figure hovered by the door, a hand pushing down the handle.

"Don't come out here," Zoe called in panic.

"Zoe?"

She rushed forward, pushing Christian back into the bedroom, nausea swirling at the shock on his face as he surveyed the blood on the carpet and saw the blood on her lace gloves and dress.

"Zoe, are you okay? What on earth?" His eyes were full of concern and love.

"There's been an accident."

Zoe let Christian hold her as she cried, but she knew she couldn't afford to cry for long. She couldn't allow herself to be weak. She had to stay strong and smart, like always.

And she would do whatever it took to keep her sister safe.

Acknowledgements

Thank you to:

Rosemary Gemmell, my writer mum, for numerous pep talks and encouragement. Excellent editorial support in the more recent final drafts, and technical support, made it possible for *Promise Me* to come out into the world.

My fiancé, Chris Andres, for unfaltering encouragement and helpful insights throughout the final drafts, and for telling me to keep going.

Writer friends who champion! Leona McPherson, for helpful feedback on the opening chapters way back at the start, and Rebecca Johnstone, for an AMAZING cover.

My friend and colleague, Hilary Wilkie, who 'career coached' me and encouraged me to move forward at a time I felt stuck.

Adjudicator, Shona MacLean, who awarded *Promise Me* second prize in the SAW Constable Award way back in 2013, and made me realise I had the start of something readable.

Judges of the Guppy Books Open Submissions Competition 2020 for short listing *Promise Me* and allowing me to keep the faith in this story. (Thanks Bella Pearson for taking the time to offer some editorial comments).

Keith Charters for editorial input in the early stages of *Promise Me*, before I took my book on a different journey.

Police and law officials who answered questions I had. Any mistakes/errors in references to procedures are all my own.

And lastly, thank you to all of the amazing readers, librarians. teachers, community workers, and my wider writing community of friends, (special mention to Kirkland Ciccone), who championed my debut Young Adult novel, *Follow Me*, and welcomed me into their world.

About the Author

Author Victoria Gemmell lives in Renfrewshire

Her debut Young Adult mystery novel *Follow Me* was published by Strident Publishing Ltd. in October 2015. *Follow Me* won the Scottish Association of Writers TC Farries Award, and is on the Scottish Book Trust list of 'Thrilling Books for Teen Readers.'

Victoria has had numerous short stories published in a variety of literary journals, and her collection of contemporary short stories (for older readers), 'Exposure' was released in November 2018.

Victoria works with teenagers on a daily basis as a careers adviser and enjoys getting to put on her 'author hat' when engaging with young people through talks and creative writing workshops.

You can find out more about Victoria at her author website and social media channels:

https://victoriagemmell.com
Twitter @VikkiGemmell
Facebook: @victoriagemmellauthor
Instagram: @vitctoriagemmellauthor

Other books by the same author:

Young Adult Novel
Follow Me

Contemporary Short Story Collection
(for older readers)
Exposure

Coming soon...

"This place you're taking me to, it sounds too good to be true. What's the catch?"
She hesitated, lowering her voice, "It's all true; the luxuries, the comfort.
"All they want in return is one little thing. Your blood."

A young adult crossover thriller
Young Blood

Held captive in a gothic house, kidnapped teenagers from the care system are exploited by a wealthy ring of powerful individuals for their 'pure plasma' blood transfusions. To cure illness and chase the dream of eternal youth, no price is too high.

When fifteen-year-old Hope goes missing, her friend Ana starts to unravel dark secrets that could lead to her rescue.

But then Ana has to make an impossible choice, receiving an offer that could mean curing her mum of early on-set dementia, at the cost of friendships and lives.

Would you betray your friends
to save your Mum?